Thirteen Shades of Black and White

Thirteen Shades
of Black and White

short fiction by

Michael Bryson

TURNSTONE PRESS

Turnstone Press
607 – 100 Arthur Street
Artspace Building
Winnipeg, Manitoba
Canada R3B 1H3
www.TurnstonePress.com

Turnstone Press gratefully acknowledges the assistance of the
Canada Council for the Arts, the Manitoba Arts Council and
the Government of Canada through the Book Publishing
Industry Development Program for our publishing activities.

Some of these stories, or versions thereof, have appeared in
*Urban Graffiti, Event, Backwater Review, paperplates, The New Quarterly,
Queen Street Quarterly, Ink, The Antigonish Review, Pottersfield Portfolio, Black
Cat #115* and *Broken Pencil.*

Original cover art by Richard Stipl: *Incident*, 1997, oil on board (20" x 16")

Cover design: Manuela Dias
Interior design: Marijke Friesen

Printed and bound in Canada by
Friesens for Turnstone Press.

Canadian Cataloguing in Publication Data

Bryson, Michael, 1968–

Thirteen shades of black and white

Short Stories.
ISBN 0-88801-236-5

I. Title.

PS8553.R97T45 1999   C813'.54   C99-920138-7
PR9199.3.B744T45 1999

To my family

Acknowledgements

Special thanks for editorial advice and encouragement: Ian Colford, Greg Cook, Naomi Diamond, Matt Firth, Barbara Gowdy, Ken Ledbetter, Eric McCormack, Ken Sparling, Jane Urquhart, David Wade, Betsy Warland, Tom Wayman. The Internet Writing Workshop. The Canada Council for funding Writers in Residence programs. All the people in Canada who struggle to publish literary periodicals. *The New Quarterly* for taking me first. Everyone at Turnstone Press, without whom this book would not exist. Richard Stipl for the cover illustration. Friends and foes who contributed in ways large and small.

Table of Contents

At Least One Good Thing

I cornered Gloria at the supermarket. I went there after school and found her. Gloria was my sister's friend. I knew what I wanted to say to her, and I walked over to her and I said it. I had said it to myself a thousand times, so it felt like nothing. It felt ordinary. Like talking to your mother. Like crossing the street. Gloria had been friends with my sister since we were kids. I had known her a long time, but things were different now. She was restocking shelves when I went up to her. She didn't say anything. Then when I said what I said, all she said was, "When?" A little curl of a smile turned at the corner of her mouth, and then she said, "When?" I was fifteen, and she was seventeen. I knew she knew I liked her. My sister knew it, too. I felt confident that she wouldn't refuse. I was through with waiting, but I wasn't ready to become her amusement. A month later, I picked a girl out at the library, took a seat beside her, and wrote what I needed to write on a sheet of paper and slid it over to her. She was a grade or two younger than me. I liked the way she looked. Her hair and her clothes. Her face was inviting. She wrote something on the paper, crumpled it, and rolled it back to

1

me. I unfurled the paper ball, and found a phone number and a name. Justine.

Justine wanted me to be her boyfriend, but I said no. That didn't stop us, though. I wanted as much as I could get, and Justine wanted it, too. There's no purpose to my telling you this. That's how it started. That was the beginning. Justine is the one who got me started writing things down. She made me think things through. I treated her bad, but I didn't realize how much until later.

I went back to Gloria because I thought I might be in love with her. She was a black girl, beautiful with dark, smooth, chocolate-coloured skin. I hadn't seen her in six months. Hadn't thought about her. Then one night I dreamed about her, and after that I couldn't stop thinking about her. I thought about what that might mean. I thought it might be love. I went to see her. I asked her if she believed in love, and she said, "No. Not really." But she didn't rule it out. She kissed me and said she hoped that I wouldn't wait so long next time. I did it with her more than with anyone and let me tell you I miss it.

Gloria didn't know what I was going to do. Nobody did. Gloria didn't know I was going to do what got me put in here. Some people thought she did. Some people thought she told me to do it, but she didn't. She didn't hear about it until later.

Justine writes me letters. The first letter said: "Write me your life." I started with the first thing I remember. I fell down the stairs when I was two. Welcome to the world, eh? Thump, thump, thump. My childhood was a lot like that. I broke my arm skateboarding, separated my shoulder playing street hockey, had stitches in my foot, my knee, my forehead. I had an allergic reaction to a bee sting that sent me to hospital when I was twelve. That bee nearly killed me. My face swelled up and I almost stopped breathing. What happened was, I was flicking bees out of a sunflower at my friend's house. The bees would land in the sunflower and we would hit them with our fingers, stun them, and they would fall on the ground and we would kill them by stepping on them. But I hit one and I didn't stun it, and it grabbed onto my hand and stung me.

We moved a lot when I was younger. My parents moved here from Newfoundland. My father came looking for work, and my mother came with my father. They never got married, though, and they weren't here too long before they split up. I was six, I think. Six or seven. I lived with my mother after that, and we moved a lot. My mother had a boyfriend and we lived with him, but then we lived on welfare. We lived in a couple of different apartments, and then we got a place in Regent's Park, a place with subsidized rent. Ontario Housing. My mother still lives there with my sister and my sister's kid. My sister used to have her own place, but she moved out when they raised the rent. I don't know where my father is any more. The last time I heard anything about him he was back in St. John's, but I'm pretty sure he left and went somewhere else, though don't ask me where, because I don't know.

Here's what happened here yesterday. Some guy got stabbed in the TV room. It was some guy I work with when I work in the kitchen. They locked us up after it happened. I was supposed to have some time in the gym, but I didn't get that, because everyone was locked up and no one was moving. I tried to do some writing, to "write my life" to Justine, but I gave up after a while. So far I've written up to the time my Mom took me and my sister to Florida. That was the time she met some guy who wanted her to smuggle drugs in her suitcase. He kept calling us at our hotel and finally we had to move out in the middle of the night and go to Miami, where my mother said she knew someone from her high school, but it turned out that this person wasn't there any more, so we got on a bus and went to Atlanta, where my mother had a second cousin or something like that. I don't know how much Justine wants to know. I just tell her what I remember.

I have a meeting with my lawyer tomorrow. He's working on an appeal on my case. I wanted him to forget about doing it, but he said that it was worth a try, even though he says my chance of getting a lighter sentence is not good. I try not to think about it. It seems like a long time ago now. It almost seems like it was someone else that did it, but I did it. I did what I did, and there's nothing that I can do about it now, so let's get on with our lives, I say. Let's move on, but some people don't want to do that, and my lawyer is one of them. My mother is another. She still keeps asking me why I did it. Why? Why? *Like I know, Mom,* I told her. Justine at least talks about the future. She says I should read books, I should get an education, I should learn how to use computers. She's got a lot of plans, but I don't know anything about that stuff. It's going to be a long time before I get out, so I don't see the point of being serious right now. I work out a lot. That's one thing I'm serious about. I like to keep in shape.

You know what I remember about my father? He had yellow teeth. He smoked like a chimney, too, but that's not what I remember. What I remember is, he had yellow teeth. When I looked at him, I was scared. Yellow teeth, man. That's traumatic, no? When people ask me if my father ever did anything for me, I tell them he scared me away from cigarettes. I don't smoke, which is pretty rare in here. My therapist asked me about my father and I told him, *all I know is he had yellow teeth.* The bastard asked me why. Why yellow teeth? *Because he smoked, man.*

"The teeth scared you?" my therapist asked.

"Yes," I said.

"The colour?"

"Yes, man. The colour. Yellow. Yellow teeth, man."

He wanted me to talk more about my father, but I didn't want to. I don't have to, if I don't want to, that's in the rules. I could say lots about my father, but why should I? I got no reason to, and I won't.

Justine asked me to write her stories about happy things. I started to write her about the time me and my friend Bill killed a cat, but I stopped and threw that story out. It's a funny story, but it isn't one Justine would like.

When the Blue Jays won the World Series, I was happy. When they won it again, I was happy again. When else was I happy? I thought hard about that, so I could come up with something to tell Justine. One thing I know for sure, I don't like Christmas. Every time Christmas comes around I end up in trouble. There's something about Christmas that makes me lose it.

I used to shoplift a lot. I got a thrill out of that. The biggest thing I ever took was a TV, one of the small ones. Actually, I didn't take it. I just played the screen, while my friend Pete took it. Pete had another friend, some guy that I didn't know, who had a car, and Pete took the TV out to the car while I diverted the salesman. I never did see the TV after that, and I never got anything from Pete for my part, either.

I decided to tell Justine about the only time I ever won anything. When I was nine or ten I was on a ball hockey team and we won the championship. We didn't have a good team, but we pulled off the win when we needed it. I set up the winning goal. When I started to write about it in my letter to Justine, all sorts of details came back to me. I remembered how I took the ball away from the defenceman and slid the ball through his legs and passed it out in front over the goalie's stick and my friend James pounded it into the back of the net. I remembered throwing my stick in the air. I almost got thrown out of the game for that. I threw my stick in the air and it almost came down on top of the referee. My mother punished me more than the referee did for that. She grounded me for a week.

Justine is going to come and see me next week. I tried to tell her to get another boyfriend, but she says she doesn't want to. "One's enough," she said. I laughed when she said that.

Justine said she's sad for me. I tried to tell her that it's okay. One thing I'm pretty sure about is that I need time to think. I never had a lot of that before, and now I do, so that's one good thing that's come out of this, I told her. At least one good thing.

Beginnings & Endings

Dave

Where did I meet her? At the coffee shop around the corner.
Why did I let her come home with me? I don't know. She had
the look of someone who needed something, and I was able
to give it at little cost to myself. She was assertive; she was
persistent; she made it seem the logical, humane choice. It
felt good hearing myself say, "Okay. Come if you want." I
only had a floor for her to sleep on, I told her. I told her she
had to leave in the morning when I left to go to work.

"Sure," she said. "It's a deal."

I don't have a big place, and I don't often have guests,
but I wasn't thinking about those things when she asked me.

"I've seen you here before," she said.

I had gone to the coffee shop to get away from a short
story I was writing. Trying to write. I had been stuck at what
I thought was the halfway point for over a week.

She was sitting at the next table, a paperback in front of
her. Atwood's *The Handmaid's Tale*, I later found out.

"You look familiar," I said.

She was wearing a green canvas army jacket over a black

7

t-shirt and a baseball cap turned backwards on her head. Familiar like any of a couple hundred others.

"What's your name?" she said.

"Dave," I said.

"Hi, Dave," she said. "I'm Darlene."

It seemed we might be at an impasse until she said, "I need a favour. I need a place to stay tonight. Could you put me up?"

"No," I said.

"It's just me," she said.

"No," I said again. I say no three times to most things. I'm not an impulsive person, to say the least.

"It's just one night," she said.

I didn't say anything to that, I just looked at her and blinked. People afterwards asked me if I wasn't afraid of her, afraid she might steal my stuff, or worse. I didn't have any thoughts like that. There had been a number of reports in the newspapers about homeless kids. The mayor had declared war on them, saying he wanted to "clean up the streets." It had mostly been background noise to me, part of the evolving urban narrative. I didn't feel connected to the mayor's battle in any way, but I have a natural tendency to identify with the underdog, so I think the mayor's war opened the window that Darlene crawled through.

"My pimp's looking for me," she said, "and I need to stay off the streets."

"Okay," I said then. "Come if you want."

Then I gave her my conditions.

"Sure," she said. "It's a deal."

DARLENE

He looked clean. He looked safe. He looked like the best option at the time. I thought that I might have seen him before, but I wasn't sure. It didn't matter much, anyway. I was beat, man. I was tired.

We went back to his place. He said it was small, and he didn't lie. The place was a one-bedroom with kind of a hallway with a TV and a futon couch in it. He pulled the couch away from the wall and unfolded it into a bed.

"I thought you said there was only the floor," I said.

"I didn't want you to come," he said.

"Oh. Good one," I said.

He went into his bedroom and came back with a sleeping bag and a pillow.

"Just don't try to sleep with me," I said.

"Don't worry," he said.

"I mean it," I said.

He nodded. "Don't worry."

"I'm not kidding," I said. "If you try anything, I'll hurt you."

That made him think.

"Darlene," he said, all serious. "If you say one more thing about that, about us not sleeping together—I'll ask you to leave."

"Just don't," I said.

"I won't."

"Okay," I said. Then I laughed. It was strange, because mostly it goes the other way. I get thrown out for not having sex.

I was feeling really tired.

Dave said he put an extra towel in the bathroom. He got me a glass of water and put it on the table beside the TV.

"Good night," he said, then he went into his room.

"Good night," I said.

I unzipped the sleeping bag and threw it over me like a blanket. I slept with my clothes on. I didn't want him to touch me. I really didn't.

DAVE

Okay, so now you know how it started.

The next day when I got up for work, Darlene was in the shower. She had already folded up the futon. I went to the kitchen and put on a pot of coffee. When she came out, she had her jacket on and her backpack thrown over her shoulder.

"Okay, thanks," she said.

She walked past me and started putting on her boots.

"Don't you want some breakfast?" I asked.

"That wasn't part of the deal," she said.

"Come on. Eat something," I said.

"Toast and coffee," she said.

I pulled a couple of apples out of the fridge and handed them to her. "For later." She put them in the front pockets of her coat. I poured her a coffee and threw two slices of bread into the toaster. I turned on the radio to listen to the news.

"Big plans for today?" I asked.

"No," she said. "You?"

I shook my head. She sipped her coffee.

We sat in silence for a minute.

She stood up. "I gotta go," she said. "Thanks for everything. Really."

Then she left. I didn't try to stop her this time. The toaster popped. I poured the rest of her coffee into the sink.

I didn't think too much about her after that. I was working towards a deadline at work and putting in a lot of overtime. I had a vacation coming up, and I was looking forward to that. I had booked a hotel room in New York City. I had never been there. I wanted to check out some famous watering holes, some of Dylan Thomas's last stops. I wanted to spend my days in art galleries and my nights in bars. I had a friend doing graduate work at Columbia, Kerouac's old stomping ground, and he had promised to scare up some women. My friend was a bit of a Beat himself.

I would like to tell you that I forgot about Darlene after she left, but that's not true. I just thought I'd never see her again. I'm the kind of guy who remembers a lot of things and wishes he didn't.

DARLENE

I left. I thought he was trying to make a move. "Big plans for today?" You know how it is.

I usually hang out downtown with the squeegees. I'm not a squeegee. Okay, sometimes I'm a squeegee. I'm not a prostitute, though. Really and truly. That line about my pimp was just a line. A line and a line only. I needed a place to sleep and, hey, it worked.

Where do you live, Darlene? I don't live nowhere now. I used to live in a squat on Spadina, but the police cleared us out. I stayed a few nights in High Park after that, but I found it creepy. Also, there was this boy there who wanted in my pants. I don't sleep with anybody, okay? Why do you think I left home? I don't want to be touched.

I've been on the streets for about six weeks. Last summer I lived on the streets, too. That was the first time. Then I got put in a foster home. Then I got put in a second foster home. I left there six weeks ago. It was summer and I had to leave. I couldn't not leave, you see what I mean? I had to go. I had itchy feet. Otherwise I would have gone crazy. I felt like that. Like I was going crazy, like I was going to explode.

I went to see my counsellor after I left Dave's place. It was the first time I had gone to see her since I left my second foster home. Her name is Carole, and I think she's all right. Mostly she just sits and listens to me. She's about the only person I know who doesn't tell me what to do. Well, she does tell me what to do sometimes, but she leaves it up to me. "It's your decision," she says a lot. "Your life." Man, that's nice to hear sometimes. You wouldn't think that would be hard to understand, but people always want to be the boss.

Carole didn't seem surprised to see me. She said she would have to tell my foster parents that I had gone to see her, but she wasn't going to force me to go back. She has a nice office. It was air-conditioned. I noticed that right away. She has art on the wall, too. Most of it is Native stuff. She explained it to me once. The paintings were about healing. They were by people who had been in the residential schools. Carole told me a little bit about that, about the Native residential schools. They don't teach you that stuff in school, man. I didn't hear nothing in school but lies.

I told Carole that I wanted another foster home. I didn't want to go back to that second place. I couldn't say for sure what was wrong with it, but I knew that I didn't want to go back. I knew I could say stuff like that to Carole. She wouldn't make me feel stupid for not having a reason.

Carole was the first person I told about my stepfather. I don't talk about him much any more. He's the reason I don't want no one to touch me. I won't tell you what he did, what we did. I don't even like to think about it.

Carole asked me if I wanted to go to the police. I said no. Not now. Not yet. I don't think I could do that. Not because of him. Because of me. I don't think I could take it. Not now. Not yet.

DAVE

In the beginning Darlene was a disruption to me. She entered the stream of my life like a pebble tossed from the shore. The surface rippled with the shock of impact. The pebble settled. The stream flowed on, navigating an altered path.

Darlene ended something and she began something; she began something and she ended something.

I saw her again the following Saturday.

DARLENE
I went down to Harbourfont. Down to the lake. I like going down there. I like watching the people. I like the buskers, the street musicians. I like watching the boats, watching the planes take off and land at the island airport. I like the breeze off the lake.

I saw Dave down there.

DAVE
She was wearing the same clothes, the same stupid baseball cap on backwards. She saw me first. I was glad to see her.

I was sitting in one of the cafés, sipping a beer, reading that Kroetsch novel. Beginnings and endings. I had them on my mind.

I waved at her to come join me.

"You want something to eat?" I asked.

"Sure," she said.

I gestured to the waitress to bring a menu. The waitress was from Ireland. She was in Toronto for the summer on an employment exchange program.

"How have you been?" I asked.

"Good," she said.

She picked up the Kroetsch novel, flipped it over. On the back cover was a photograph of Kroetsch from the 1960s. He looked awful, like a real suit. Some kind of McCarthyesque dinosaur. He wasn't like that at all, I knew. But that's what he looked like. Like a university lecturer. A real drag.

Darlene pointed at the photograph.

"Creepy," she said.

"Isn't it awful?" I agreed.

She set the book back on the table, photograph side down.

"Do you read?" I asked.

She reached into her backpack and pulled out *The Handmaid's Tale*, the Atwood novel I'd seen her with in the coffee shop.

The waitress arrived with the menu.

I picked up *The Handmaid's Tale* and flipped through it while Darlene perused the menu. I figured I had read maybe half of Atwood's novels. I hadn't read *The Handmaid's Tale*. I saw the movie. I hadn't felt inclined to read the book.

The waitress came back and Darlene ordered.

"You're paying, right?" she asked me.

I nodded. "Yes."

Darlene ordered and the waitress left. I asked Darlene what she was doing down here.

"I like to watch the people," she said. "People down here always seem happy."

I hadn't thought about that before, but it was true. Coming down to the water was like a return to childhood. Coming down to the water signalled a carefree day. It helped to create a sunny disposition.

I took a sip of beer.

DARLENE

"Do you read?" he asked me.

I think maybe Dave's okay.

I started telling him about what I'd done after I left his place. I told him a little about Carole. I told him I wanted another foster home. I told him this was my second summer on the streets. I told him I wasn't a prostitute. I wanted him to know that. I didn't have a pimp, and nobody was looking for me. At least I didn't think there was. My foster parents might be looking for me, but I don't think so.

"You're bright," he said. "And you're cute," he said.

"Are you hitting on me?" I asked. I wasn't afraid of him no more. I just wanted to be sure.

14

"No," he said. "I'm just saying what I see. You've got strength and you're working things through, I can tell."

He tapped his head when he said that.

Working things through.

"You're a survivor. You'll do well."

"I don't bend," I said. I meant it.

"Bending's not good," he said, "though there's a certain type of man who likes women like that."

"What type of man?" I asked.

"Men who work in advertising," he said.

He smiled when he said that. I wasn't sure if he was kidding or what.

DAVE

I met a woman in New York. I was at the Metropolitan Museum of Art. She was small, dark, European. She came up to me with her program. She wanted me to tell her how to get to the Warhols. I don't know why but I said, "I'll take you there, but first come with me for coffee."

She came. We talked. We saw the Warhols. We went out for dinner. She was a secretary for a modelling agency. It was her day off. She took me to a small club where they played jazz, authentic ancient ragtime. She smoked cigarettes through a filter. She wore a fur around her neck. She looked like pictures I'd seen of Jackie Kennedy. It might have been the 1960s—or the 1930s. She kissed me and gave me her business card. I never called her. I don't know why, except I was sure we had already been to the mountaintop. It doesn't get any better than that.

I never saw Darlene again, either. I look for her when I'm downtown or when I'm in the coffee shop where I first met her. I hand out quarters to street kids more frequently now. I don't worry about her. Beginnings and endings. It's best not to get them confused.

DARLENE

I could tell you some things. I could tell you things that would keep you up at night, but I'm not going to.

Just read the newspapers.

RUNNING WITH THAT INDIAN

"So, Barry," Dad said, fumbling with his cigarette. He was in
his wheelchair, wearing a blue hospital robe. Barry and I
were on a park bench. I found it hard to look at my father,
his pride hurt so bad.

"You work at the casino, am I right?" Dad asked.

"I'm in construction," Barry said.

"You work for Macleans?"

"Used to," Barry said. "I started my own company a
couple years ago." *Got to keep the money on the reserve*, I had
often heard him say.

I had tried to keep Barry away from my father for as
long as I could. After the casino appeared three years ago, he
tore into nearly every Indian person he met. *That casino will
be the downfall of the entire region*, I had heard him intone to
his nurse just the other day. I was concerned about what he
might say to Barry. My kids adored Barry, and I didn't want
anything to upset him, to infect our relationship. Of course,
Barry is one of the most level-headed people I've ever met,
so my concern was really about myself. That was something

that I was starting to learn. It was my anxiety, and I needed to take responsibility for how I dealt with it.

Dad asked, "You working on anything right now?"

"A community centre. Up on the reserve," Barry said.

"Is that right?"

"Next month we put the spade in the ground on a place for our seniors."

"Jimmy Pike's got a room booked there, Dad," I pitched in.

"Is that right?"

Jimmy had been one of my father's fishing buddies years ago.

"A place just for Indian old folks." Dad dropped his eyes and shook his head, and I thought he looked suddenly lost, like he was searching for a fixed place in the shifting corridors of his mind. He seemed so sad. So tired. Then he lifted his face, turned to Barry and, pointing his cigarette at him, said, "Why do you people always need to do things off on your own, all by yourselves? I've never been able to understand that." He didn't say it like he was angry; more like a whisper. Like he was talking to us from the other end of a long tunnel.

I looked at Barry. He had a smile on his face.

"Your Dad's not so bad," he said later when we stopped for coffee on our way back to my place.

"He's not the man he used to be," I said.

"He's a fighter," Barry said. "I admire that."

Dad was in the hospital because he had a fall. He broke his hip. He had been living at home alone, but that wasn't going to be possible any more. My mother died two years ago and my father had been on a downward slide ever since.

Barry asked, "Am I going to see you Friday?"

"Sure," I said. I gave my kids to their father every second weekend and took myself and my dog over to Barry's place. Barry had a place on the edge of the reserve, back in the woods, isolated.

I put my hand over his hand and we locked fingers.

"Kiss me," I said.

Barry leaned across the table and planted one on me. I liked it when Barry kissed me in public. I'd heard stories about how a couple of band members didn't like me staying over at Barry's, and when he kissed me I felt less insecure.

"I want you to stop running with that Indian."

The message on my machine when I got home was from Dad. I was glad that my kids didn't get to it first.

"I want it to stop," the message said. "I don't want any daughter of mine running around with no Indian."

Barry was Mr. Fearless. He left school when he was sixteen, took off with a pair of buddies to Toronto. Then someone told him about the Mohawks in New York City, how they worked the big construction sites, walking the high beams on the skyscrapers. It's a little like flying, he once said to me. It made him feel like an eagle. He was up there alone—and free. He said he was never afraid of anything after that.

Barry came back from New York five years after he left. I was married by then. Knocked up, too. I remember running into him at the video store and thinking that he looked real good, happy. I had a sweet spot for him that went back to high school. I used to talk to him when I saw him, and when my husband left he started coming around to cut the grass, fix the car and trim the trees, which didn't take long to lead to other things.

I called to tell him about my father's message, but he wasn't home.

My father was a big man, a strong man in his time. He'd worked in the woods in his younger days, cutting trees, fighting fires. It took my mother to get him to settle down. He used to manage the arena when I was just little. Then he took over the movie theatre with a pal. A couple of times since he's been in hospital he's called me 'Sharon,' which was my mother's name. The first time he did that I corrected him.

"It's Debbie, Dad," I said. "Debbie."

"Of course," he said. Then he asked me about my brother, Bob, but I don't have a brother. Bob's my uncle, and he's dead.

I did my best to talk to my kids about their grandfather. I wanted them to know that he loved them, even if he couldn't say so.

My daughter had begun having nightmares. She would wake up screaming, and when I came running she would tell me she had dreamed her granddad had died.

"No, sweetie," I told her. "It's okay. Your granddad's okay."

I told Barry I thought my daughter was reliving the trauma of when her father had left.

"That's possible," he said. "Or maybe her grandfather's spirit goes for walks in the night."

I poked him. "Don't give me any of that Indian bullshit," I said.

Barry laughed. He was a trickster if I ever met one.

I decided to tell my kids about my father's phone message about Barry. I didn't like to be the one bringing trouble into my kids' lives, but I wanted to make them strong and I figured the only way to do that was to show them I could stand up to my troubles, too. We could stand up to them together.

When my husband left, I wasn't much use as a mother. This is hard for me to admit, and someday I'll tell my kids it was all I could do to save myself. I had felt for a while that my husband wasn't happy, but I never thought he would leave. A couple of friends had tried to tell me he was having an affair, but I thought they were just jealous. That sounds strange I know, but it's true. Denial is a powerful force; it works hard to shield you from the stuff that would destroy you. It's got limits, though, and when I hit them, I faced the pain with 'hope in my heart' and found a way out the other side.

"How is he doing?"

"Better," the nurse said. "His attitude seems to have improved."

It was going to be weeks, though, I knew, before he was on his feet again, which meant more valleys than peaks, I was sure.

I was looking for a bed for him in a nursing home, but with all the cutbacks—well, none was available. The hospital would keep him until he regained his feet, but after that they were threatening to send him home with me, an eventuality I felt in no way ready to accept.

After the nurse left, I stood outside his room, thinking about what it would be like after he was gone. My life had seen so many changes. This was more than just another one. I stepped into the room. He was sleeping. I pictured him again on my wedding day, how happy he had been. I saw the smile that lit up his face when he teased my kids. I remembered how he had held me in his powerful arms longer than usual on the day of my mother's funeral, how I had felt him shake, how I had seen his frailty that day, understood his vulnerabilities in a way I hadn't before, though he'd done his best to hide them.

I got Barry on the phone. "He's at it again. Only worse."

"What happened?"

I wasn't sure I wanted to tell him.

"He said things about my mother," I said. "About when they were younger."

"Like what?" Barry asked.

I hesitated. "Okay," I said. "I'll tell you."

I took a sip from the glass of wine I'd poured myself after I got home from the hospital. "He said my mother used to have an Indian boyfriend when he was off in the woods in the summers. He said my mother used to go up to the reserve to get drunk and carry on. 'I don't want you turning out like that,' he said. He's lost it, Barry."

Barry didn't say anything.

I took another sip of wine. I felt awful.

Barry told me a story once about what it meant to be Indian. He said he was travelling in New Brunswick, hitchhiking, when he got picked up by this guy who used to be a priest. Barry asked this guy why he'd dropped out of the priesthood, and the guy said he'd been evangelizing in Toronto, going door to door, and he'd met a woman who had been at Auschwitz. She showed him the serial number tattooed on her arm. "Christians did this to me," she said. "Please leave." The priest told Barry the experience had led to a breakdown in his faith.

He asked Barry, "You're Native?"

"That's right," Barry said.

"What the church did to your people wasn't right," the guy said. Then he apologized over and over, until Barry told him it was okay.

I told you Barry is a joker. "I'll tell you some words my Elder told me before I left home," he told the former priest. Then he said: "He not busy being born is busy dying."

Barry came to pick me up as usual on Friday after I dropped my kids off at their father's.

"I didn't think you were coming," I said.

"Why not?"

"I don't know, I just didn't." I didn't have anything packed.

Barry had his arms around me, his hands under my shirt. He kissed me and I held on to him. I held on to him like I would never let him go.

DAY TWO, SASKATCHEWAN

The kid was asleep, so I poked him.

"Look."

"What?" His eyes were still closed.

One lid came up, then the other. He looked across me and out the window. Red, orange, and yellow layers of sky piled on the horizon. He turned to his left, stared out over more fields, more sky.

"We're surrounded," he said.

"You got it, kid."

"Can I go back to sleep now?"

We were two days out of Vancouver. We were going to Toronto.

"Sleep, kid," I said. His eyes were already closed. He wasn't much of a talker: nine years old, a little sullen, unkempt. I took another view out the window. The world has a lot to offer; that's what I wanted to teach the kid. The world has a lot to offer if you know where to look.

It had been three years since my last trip to the prairies. I spent a summer in Saskatoon, living with a woman named Laura. I met her in California, where she was living on the

beach, sleeping under a bridge with the son of a bank
president, spending her days surfing and chasing down
tourists for spare change. She had gone south looking for an
acting job. She told me she took off her clothes a couple of
times for money ("hey, Marilyn Monroe did it"). I was taking
the kid to see her. I was hoping for a reconciliation.

When we were in Calgary, I told the kid about Laura.
He wanted to know if I loved her. His mother had drilled
that word into him. Love, the bonding agent. Love, all-
powerful, everlasting. I'd known his mother for a long time,
and she was always like that.

"Yes, I love her," I confessed to the kid. I wasn't sure if I
did or not. After I left I wrote, and she wrote back.

My confession exhausted the topic. The kid asked about
Toronto.

I told him about SkyDome and the ferries that cross the
harbour to the islands that ring the bay. I told him about
Casa Loma and the subway system and the Eaton Centre
and Yonge Street and the time that I saw Wayne Gretzky at
Maple Leaf Gardens.

"Big deal," he said. "I saw Eric Lindros."

His father had taken him to see the Canucks and the
Flyers. The kid enjoyed hockey.

"The Hall of Fame is in Toronto," I said.

He wanted to make it our first stop.

The bus cut a line across the prairie. I lay back in my
seat and tried to sleep.

II

The week before I left Laura the rain was heavy. A tornado
tore through a farm south of the city, leaving three small
girls orphans. I quit my job at a pub, where I had been
working in the kitchen. Over the previous weeks, Laura had
repeatedly accused me of sleeping with Dorothy, a waitress

where I worked. I quit to put an end to the harassment, but it didn't stop.

"Who do you like most at your work?" she had asked after I had been at the pub going on six weeks.

I didn't understand the depth of the question.

"Dorothy," I said. Dorothy was an artist. She had a showing coming up. She sought me out after I had shown an interest in her work.

When the time came for Dorothy's showing, Laura fell ill.

She sunk into bed, bathed in blankets, a hot-water bottle pressed to her chest.

"You go."

Then: "Was it good? What was the slut wearing?"

A week later I left town. I wrote an apology to Laura when I got to Vancouver, and she responded with a series of flaming letters that eventually mellowed. The words never stopped, and I began to wonder if we owed ourselves a second chance.

III

The bus pulled into Saskatoon as the city began to shake itself awake, the dusty streets largely barren, a mist rising off the river.

I bought us breakfast at the coffee shop in the bus depot. The kid took a sip of my coffee and pronounced it livable. He reminded me then of my brother. He has his eyes, his quiet manner, his puckishness, even though he doesn't have any of my brother's blood in him. The kid's mother is my sister-in-law. That's how I think of her, anyway, even though she never married my brother. They were teenagers, crazy in love, when he died. She survived the car accident that killed him. Within two years she was married and pregnant.

The kid sometimes called me "Uncle," but most of the time he just called me Jake.

27

I stuffed our bags in a locker at the bus station and walked the kid downtown. The city looked the same as when I'd left it. A few new stores had opened, a few had closed down.

"What does she look like?" the kid asked when we got to the park by the river.

"Laura?"

The kid nodded. "Is she pretty?"

"Yes," I said. "She's beautiful."

"What does she do?" he asked.

"She's an actress."

"In movies?"

"In plays," I said.

I didn't tell him that she was actually working as a secretary for a friend of her father. I also didn't tell the kid that I was hoping to convince Laura to quit her job and come with us to Toronto. If she wouldn't do that, then I was hoping at least for a warm reunion, something that would suggest we could start over again after I dropped the kid back in Vancouver.

The water in the river was low and a sandbar had formed about twenty yards offshore. The kid wanted to walk out to it, the water wasn't deep, but I didn't want him to get wet.

"We'll come back later," I promised. "After lunch, we'll get your bathing suit and you can splash around all you want."

IV

Listen, I know it might seem strange for a grown man to be travelling with someone else's child. Like I said, though, the kid reminds me of my brother, and I treat him with respect, and we get along fine. It's coming up on twelve years since my brother's death, a lifetime, really. I was in my first year of university, preparing for final exams, when it happened. I never went back to school.

My brother was the kind of guy that everybody liked. I'm not saying that he didn't piss me off sometimes, because he sure did. He knew how to hit me best, how to really get to me, and I had to thump him hard a couple of times, but I loved him more than I loved anyone, I think. I say that because after he died I didn't love anyone for a long time, and the people that I've loved since I've loved in a different way.

My brother's girlfriend, the kid's mother, lived across the street from us. She used to drop by to talk to my mother, whom she trusted like an older sister. She invited all of us to her wedding, but I didn't go. At the last minute I decided it wasn't right. The wedding made me think too much of my brother and the grief I still felt. Like Hamlet, I wanted to stop the wedding, but I didn't.

The next couple of years I drifted. I moved to Toronto, Halifax, Montréal, Thunder Bay before hitching to California, where I wanted to learn to surf. I had plans to write a book of poetry and a screenplay, but those things never happened.

When I hooked up with Laura I was making my money by working in a bookshop and selling grass on the side. The set-up made me paranoid, I was constantly afraid of getting arrested, and I was glad when Laura said she had been thinking about moving home. We settled into an apartment off Broadway in Saskatoon in late May and I was out of there by the end of August. We had been together less than six months, but I left thinking we could have had something good. We could have pulled it out with a little effort. That's what I tried to tell Laura in my letters after I left, and by the time I hopped on the bus with the kid in Vancouver I was half convinced Laura was ready to try again. I didn't tell her I was coming, though, and that might have been a tactical mistake. I had thought I would have a better chance if I surprised her. Who's to say?

V

I parked the kid in a booth at the Dairy Queen and went outside to call Laura from a pay phone. I was hoping to catch her before she went to work.

The phone rang. She answered.

"Hello?"

"Hi, Laura. It's Jake." We hadn't spoken since I left.

"Jake, my god," she said flatly. "Where are you?"

"I'm here," I said. "In Saskatoon, outside the Dairy Queen downtown. I came to see you."

"I don't think so."

"I have the kid with me," I told her. She knew about the kid. I had written about him in my letters. I had told her I half considered him my son.

"Oh, Jake," she said. "Your timing is terrible."

"Can we stay with you tonight, at least? The kid needs a place to sleep. He's exhausted from the bus."

"Jake, Jake," she said. "Call me after work, okay? I can't make any decisions now."

Then she hung up.

The kid and I spent most of the day walking up and down the path beside the river. We took in a display at the art gallery, which was hosting an exhibit of prairie landscape painters. *The painters demonstrate in their work the struggle for the individual to encounter in its totality the vast scope of prairie landscape*, the display copy with the exhibit said. I thought the paintings in the exhibit were brilliant, but the kid was less impressed.

In the afternoon I took the kid back to the sandbar and let him splash around in the water, then we had a nap in the shade of some bushes.

All day I considered what to do about Laura. Did I want to try again? I called when I was sure that she would be home from work, but before we were even a minute into the conversation, she said she didn't want to see me again.

"I've met someone, Jake."

"When?"

"A while ago."

"You never said."

"I know. I should have, but I didn't know if it was going to work out."

"And it is?" I asked.

"Jake, I'd rather not discuss it with you."

"Okay. All right."

"I'm sorry, Jake. I hope you find somewhere to stay. I just don't think that I should see you."

"Okay," I repeated.

"I'm sorry, Jake," she said again.

I said, "Then I guess this is goodbye."

"Goodbye, Jake."

Goddamn, I thought. I hung up the phone. The kid was standing outside the phone booth in his swim trunks, a beach towel wrapped around his shoulders.

"We're not going to see Laura," I told him as we walked back to the bus depot to pick up our things.

"Why not?" he asked.

"That's the way things go sometimes," I said.

"I wanted to see her," he said.

"I know," I said. "And I'm sure that she wanted to see you, but it's not possible this time."

He ruminated on this for a minute.

"That's sad," he said.

I figured we had another five or six hours of sunlight. By morning we could be in Winnipeg.

SOMETHING IN THE WATER

It was Saturday night and Bob wanted to go to the ballet.

"No hockey tonight?" asked his wife.

"Let's do something different," said Bob. "I feel like a change. How about you?"

Sheila didn't know what to tell him. She was looking forward to the game. Toronto and Montréal. The big rivalry. The teams didn't often meet these days. What with all those American teams in the league now. But she knew she had often scolded Bob because they never did anything different, and now here he was offering to take her out—and to the ballet, no less.

"Okay, Bob," she said. "Sounds like a great idea."

But that wasn't how she felt the next week when Gretzky was in town and Bob wanted to see a play. Shakespeare, too. In the costumes of the period. My god, she thought. And miss the Great One. It wasn't every day he came to the Gardens. But Bob insisted. "A play is the thing," he said, and laughed like he'd said something funny.

They made their way to the theatre, which had been carved out of an old warehouse in the city's west end. Sheila settled into her chair and tried to keep up with the action. Kings, queens, princes, old school chums, ghosts. She had a hard time putting it all together. Then, halfway through the second act, she fell asleep. Bob didn't wake her until the intermission was almost over.

"I can't believe you did that," she said as they made their way to the parking lot afterwards. "All those people were looking at me."

Bob nodded timidly. He wanted to ask her what she thought of the production. Weren't the accents wonderful? Such language! But Sheila found the hockey game on the radio, and they drove home in silence. The Leafs were down by three.

"Hockey next week," Sheila said as they pulled into their driveway.

"Yes, dear," said Bob. "Hockey next week."

"Toronto's in Pittsburg," she said, hoping to revive his excitement. But Bob didn't respond, so she punched him affectionately on the shoulder. "I thought you liked Mario."

"Who?"

"Lemieux. Mario Lemieux," she said.

"I do," he said. "Mario's terrific, the best."

"He makes his whole team better," Sheila agreed cheerfully.

The following Saturday Lemieux picked up six assists, but the television entertained only one of them.

"Mario sure is a great playmaker," Sheila told Bob as they prepared for bed. Bob had decided to catch up on his reading. Kafka, Nabokov, Colette, Voltaire. Earlier in the week, he had stopped at a used bookstore on Bloor on his way home from work and filled up his briefcase. So many books, so little time. He was toying with the idea of registering for an evening course in creative writing. Maybe he could arrange a sabbatical. He started writing poetry on his lunch hour and found he had a flair for it. In another couple of months, he figured, he would have enough for a collection.

He told his wife he was glad she enjoyed the game.

"What's gotten into you?" she asked, as they slipped under the covers. She snuggled up next to him and slipped her hand under his shirt. His skin felt cold, clammy.

"Oh, Sheila."

"Bob."

He rolled over on his back, but she found him unready.

"Is something the matter, Bob?"

He shook his head. He wanted to make her happy, but it was too soon. He felt guilt creep up his spine.

"Hold me, Sheila," he said. "Just hold me."

But she withdrew to her side of the bed.

"Sheila, don't be like that."

"It's Saturday night, Bob."

"I know."

"Well, you should know, then."

"Just hold me, Sheila. Don't go so fast."

But she pulled back the covers and reached for her sweater.

"I'm going to get a drink," she said sharply. "Do you want anything? Scotch? Gin? Vodka?"

"Gin," he said. It used to be his favourite, but he had no taste for it now. Sheila was going to have something, so he thought he better have something. He wanted her to be happy.

Sheila fetched the drinks, and Bob sat up in bed. He thought about removing his pyjamas. Would the sight of his naked body help the process of reconciliation with his wife? He thought not. He picked a book of Nabokov's short stories off his bedside table, flipped through it, and tossed it on the floor. What was getting into him? Something was different. Different, but better. He felt close to his wife, closer than he ever had before. He felt an urge to talk about their relationship. He had been reflecting on how they had met, what had drawn them to each other, how each complemented the other. A remarkable synergy existed

between them. That was his conclusion. He and Sheila
shared a extraordinary energy. He wanted to talk to her
about it. He felt their love had moved into greater depths
these past few weeks. Their love was rich as one of those
triple chocolate cakes. He fluffed his pillow.

"What do you think about children, Sheila?" he asked
when she returned.

"Bob, please!"

She handed him his drink and slid into bed beside him.

"You *are* strange all of a sudden," she said.

She raised her glass to his and leaned over to kiss him.

"Here's to our childless marriage," she said. They
touched their glasses lightly together.

The following Tuesday, Sheila brought home a computer. Bob
had been after her for six months to buy one, but Sheila had
always managed to persuade him they had other priorities.

He asked, "Did we discuss this?"

But Sheila pretended not to hear. "Get me the scissors,
will you? I need to cut open this box. And clear away a space
on the desk."

Bob bit his tongue and stepped into the kitchen to whip
up a salad. Sheila put on one of Bob's Rolling Stones CDs
and began to hook up their new computer. Bob finished the
salad and opened a can of soup. Sheila turned on the
computer and called for Bob to examine their new appliance.
Bob set the soup on simmer and ventured into the other
room. He couldn't have been less excited than if Quebec had
voted to separate. He saw that this instrument would come
between them. Sheila had brought divisiveness into their
house. She had taken a step he wasn't prepared to follow.

"It's great, Sheila," he said.

"You like it?"

"Oh, yes."

Days passed into weeks. Weeks passed into months. Sheila spent more and more time with their computer, holding it, stroking it. Bob turned to his parents. His father in particular. They started to spend hours on the phone, and every other day they found an excuse to meet for coffee. They had problems to discuss, relationships to mend. Could you believe the trouble their friends got into? Then there was the violence that seeped out of the house next door and the romantic lives of popular entertainers. So much to talk about.

"Did you hear about the neighbour's son?" Bob's dad asked.

"No."

"His wife is beating him again."

"That's terrible. Someone should stop her."

Bob had never felt so close to his father. They had made a breakthrough, but something had gotten into Mom. She had bought herself a motorcycle jacket and was talking about taking lessons from the Harley Davidson dealer.

"It's her second childhood," Bob's dad said. "She says I'm not exciting any more. She flirts with the boys behind the counter at McDonald's. She disappears in the afternoons and won't tell me where she goes. I think she's seeing Bruce, our mechanic. I heard her say to her friend Jean how she'd like to tune his engine."

Bob sighed and wondered why it was so hard for women to acknowledge their feelings of inadequacy. Why was it necessary for women to act out their anxieties in such maladjusted ways? On his way home he stopped at the flower shop. He was considering planting a rose bush in the corner of their yard. As he admired the plants a vanload of teenage girls drove past. One of the girls leaned out the window and yelled at Bob: "Long live the snake!" One of the other girls let loose with a sharp wolf whistle. Bob stood in front of the flower shop, shaking his head.

Girls will be girls, he thought.

He picked out a rose with a dark pink hue. He took it inside the shop and charged it to Sheila's credit card. He knew exactly where he was going to put it. The very exact spot.

LIGHT AND SILVER

I was in London the week the IRA resumed its bombing campaign, ending eighteen months of peace. Donna, the Australian I had been chasing around Europe for the previous six weeks, dragged me to the scene.

"Bloody marvellous," she said, when we saw the skeleton of a building left behind by the bomb. The police kept us from getting close, but we saw enough. Donna trained her long lens on the shattered ruins and shot half a roll of film. It was amazing, the destruction. I thought of Oklahoma City, the front of the federal building blown off by reconstituted fertilizer.

We spent the afternoon in Hyde Park, then tramped over to Buckingham Palace, where Donna took pictures of the soldiers and their machine guns.

A week later a bomb tore the insides out of a double-decker bus in the theatre district, not far from the Unicorn, a pub Donna and I frequented. Donna rushed off to that site, too, but I spent the day touring the British Museum. She called the hostel where we were staying later in the day to say she wouldn't be back that night. The wreckage still sat in the street when I met her at the Unicorn the next day for lunch.

At the Unicorn she sits with a sharply dressed young man.
Peter, the Croatian poet and refugee.

"He's writing a play," she says. "About the war. But he
really wants to write a novel."

Peter nods. He is clean–shaven with remarkably strong
features: high cheekbones, solid jawline, deep, penetrating eyes
with a softness around the edges. Donna says she bumped into
him on a street corner. She asked him for directions but soon
realized he wasn't a native. Peter was a journalist, a translator.
He spoke four languages and dreamed of being a novelist. He
was living with friends in St. John's Wood.

He leans across the table, ignoring me, and takes
Donna's hand.

"You should come take pictures in Croatia," he says. "I
would show you good places."

"But there's a war on," I say.

He leans back in his chair. "There are many wars," he says.

I ask him what he means.

"In your country, you are fighting the French."

"You've been misled."

"The French are," he says, pausing to find the right
word, "separate, yes? They desire to be separate."

"Our prime minister is French," I say, but I don't think
he hears me.

"The French desire a country," he says.

"Some do."

"And the Aborigines," says Donna.

"Excuse me?"

"The Aborigines. You have them in Canada, too. Like in
Australia," she says. "They want their land back, so they can
live like they did before."

I'm not sure what to say.

Then Peter says, "So you see, you also have wars."

I let it pass, ask Peter where he's from. I ask him to tell me about his country. Europe intrigues me, though I'm not a scholar by any means.

Peter lights a cigarette and tells his story. He talks about the hills around his village back home, the valleys where he played as a kid, and the goats, and the sheep, and the priest who taught him English and who pushed him to get an education. No one in his family was educated, but the priest supplied a scholarship and persuaded his family to let him travel to the city. It's a fascinating tale, and I'm drawn into the rustic scenes and the images of the villagers who eventually shunned him and his book learning.

"In the city I met so many people, so many different people. I was amazed," he says. "I used to go to the market just to see all the people. At the school, we talked about poetry. It was the first time for me. I saw that the world was a big, big place, and I wanted to see all of it. I read about so many places and I wanted to go to them all. I was like a flower that has been hidden from the sun. I grew very fast when I was set in the light."

We order food and drinks. Peter keeps talking. He tells us about the war and the fate of the community of artists in the city where he lived.

"We had marvellous theatre. Many painters, many writers," he remembers. "We were Serb, Muslim, and Croat, all together. We believed in each other. The war was a disease that destroyed us."

He pauses and lifts a forkful of English salmon into his mouth.

"It must have been terrible," I say. When I was in public school I sat beside a Vietnamese boy who had fled with his family. They were boat people, and I heard how they climbed aboard a barge with hundreds of others and drifted in the ocean for days. They were attacked by pirates, looted, forced to land on a deserted island, and marched at gunpoint to a refugee camp.

Peter reaches for the ketchup.

"What happened to your friends?" I ask.

"Some left," he says. "Some joined the fighting. Some tried to go on like before, but the war flooded the city. It went into every crack and filled up every basement, every cabinet, every closet. No place could escape it. No one evaded it. Everything changed. The beauty of the city was ruined. We tried not to give up hope, but we knew everything we had worked for, everything we had built, was gone."

"Then you left?"

"No. I stayed. I was in love. My lover refused to go, so I stayed. We hung onto what we could. We waited to die. We were very happy together, but—it did not last."

I wait for more, but Peter says nothing. We eat in silence. I catch a glance of the television news. The police think one of the people killed in the bus explosion was the bomber. The blast appears to have been an accident, the news announcer says. The bus was not the intended target.

"Grand," says the bartender.

"Fucking pathetic terrorists," says a customer.

I look again at Peter, but he's not watching the news.

"I would like to ask you something," he says.

"Sure."

"Tell me about Canada. I read a book—I don't know." And he pauses to rest his forehead in the palm of his hand and strum the top of his head with his fingers. "Alice Munro," he says eventually. "A book about women and girls."

"*Lives of Girls and Women*," I say.

"Is that it? Yes. You're right."

"You read that?"

"Yes," he says. "I met a woman from Canada. She was in my country, helping the victims of the war. Before she went home, I asked her to send me Canadian books. She sent me this one by Alice Munro. I have not talked to anyone about it. You are the first Canadian I have met since I read it."

"Did you like it?" I ask.

"Yes. Of course," he says. "But the question is more than liking or not liking. Alice Munro has written a very interesting book. I like it because it is interesting, but I don't know your country, so I do not understand everything."

"Canada is a confusing country," I say.

"I do not understand why you say this."

"Alice Munro sees only a small part of a big country," I say. "Canada is too large for any writer."

He nods.

"Yes, perhaps. Yugoslavia was too small. Canada is too big," he concurs. "But there is more, I think. The question is more complicated."

"What is the question?"

"Yes. I don't know," he says. "Maybe it is something I cannot say. I will try." And he does, but it takes him ten minutes to find his words, and even then he apologizes for not being clear. "There is more I want to say, but I cannot. I am different here." He taps the table with his fist. "In London, I am a different person. I find it hard to talk about what I know how to talk about. I am confusing you, I know, but I am confusing myself as well. The world changes, you see? We are not the same. Time changes us. Place changes us. These are things I did not understand when I left my village."

Donna reaches under the table and pulls her camera out of her bag. Peter glances at her as she attaches her flash, but he keeps talking. Donna trains the camera on him, fiddles with the light meter and adjusts the aperture.

"What I want to know," he says, "is what you think of Alice Munro. I want to know about Canada. How do you live together? I am the son of a farmer. Now I live in the city. I do not know how to live any more. My country does not exist. Many things are possible, but I feel like I cannot move. There is a word for this. I feel—"

"Paralysed," I say, and at that moment Donna takes his picture. The flash explodes and the patrons grumble.

"Hey. We'll have none of that," demands the bartender.

"Sorry," says Donna.

But Peter continues. "Paralysed, yes," he says, undisturbed by the flash. As if it hadn't happened. "I am stopped. I am in the past. The future is far away. I feel like I will never get there. I want to know about Canada because you have vision. You see in life new ways."

"That's flattering," I say.

But he insists he's serious.

I hesitate. Too long, perhaps. His face drops, the expectation drained out of it.

"I told him about Australia," Donna interrupts. "I told him about you. He wanted to meet you, so I suggested he come today."

"Oh, I see," I say. "You should have warned me. I would have prepared something."

"I'm not sure I can help," I say to Peter. "I don't know much about Alice Munro."

"It's not about her," he says.

"I know."

He nods and glances at his watch.

"It's okay," he says after a moment. "I must go now. We will meet again, I think. And I will be more clear next time."

He pushes his chair back, stands up and strides to the bar to pay for his lunch.

Donna and I met in Prague. I was teaching English. She was passing through. We shared a coffee in a café and she asked me about good sites to photograph around the city. My teaching term was drawing to a close, so we made plans to travel together. A week later, one of my students gave me a bottle of wine. Homemade, he said. From his family in the country. That evening I gave Donna a walking tour of my neighbourhood. She talked about her travels and the book she hoped to make out of her photographs. I told her about my students and the stories I had heard about life before the Velvet Revolution. I made a point of mentioning the wine, and she agreed to share it. We talked through the night, exploring. Layer after layer fell away, each labyrinth was resolved. In the moments before the dawn, the last puzzle fell away.

"Look, Daniel, the sun."

"I see it," I said, stroking her face. Such a face. The new day reflected off her cheeks. Words had been spilt by the thousands. Our bodies at last exposed. We rolled into bed, wrapped ourselves around each other, sucked and touched, nuzzled and caressed. Later we would board trains, tour museums, sleep in discarded discos, lunch on the Left Bank, fuck in a field in the south of France as the sun set and the world turned and the emerging stars signalled what seemed only too clearly to be the clockwork perfection of the universe.

Donna documented our journey. A film school dropout and daughter of a clergyman, she loved her camera. Light and silver, she said. That's all she needed. If the pen is mightier than the sword, and a picture is worth a thousand words, well, we know who wins. Through her viewfinder, the world spoke to her. She saw photographs before they happened, like a hockey player who anticipates the play and passes the puck to where his teammate isn't, but will be soon. She watched scenes develop and placed herself where she needed to be. Click! And she had the story. Click! The magic could be transformed, reproduced, shared. It took me a long time to see what Donna saw, and I'm sure I never understood it all. She used to point at people. "Look at him, the man across the street. Waiting at the bus stop. I wonder where he's going?" Everyone had a story, a future, a past. She had a way of seeing the potential in people and amplifying it, making them seem larger than they were. Every life was enormous to her, every anecdote significant. I had spent nearly a year in Europe, running away from school, escaping my disillusionment, and she refuelled me. Her passion allowed me to move beyond my professors and their theories, and reconnect to life. Sounds grandiose, I know. But after two years at one of the top universities in the country, I felt myself sinking in a sea of abstractions—and Donna's photography allowed me to see the concrete in the mutability of the everyday.

"Peter's friends have a darkroom," she says, completing the story of the night before. We linger in the Unicorn over coffee and cigarettes. I'm glad to have her alone.

"You should see my shots," she says. "I got some great ones of you."

I ask her to show me, but she says she left them back at the house. She left her things there. She has to go back. She asks me if I remember Amsterdam. I nod.

"By the wharf?"

"Yes."

"I have a shot of you looking out over the harbour." She's smiling and looking at me. "It's good," she says, gleaming. Our knees touch under the table. "I like what it says about you. So calm, so deep, contemplative, complex. So cute, too." She laughs. Last night was the first night we had spent apart since we left Prague. I want to tell her how much I missed her, how I dreamed about her cheeks, how I'd forgotten how beautiful she was. But I don't. I want to lean across the table and kiss her. But I don't do that, either. I want to ask her about our future. For six weeks we have been living in the present. No troubles, no temptation. Every second a work of art. But a space has opened between us. The current has skipped a beat. It sounds stupid. We were apart less than twenty-four hours. Not even a complete rotation of the planet, but for a month and a half we have functioned as one organism, and last night I felt her peel away from me. Donna, come back, I want to say, but she would scold me for being melodramatic. Here I am, sweetheart. Here I am, lover. Right here before you. I'm not going anywhere. I'm right here for you, my love.

We leave the pub. The bombed crust of the bus is still sitting like a gravestone in the middle of the street. People pass it on the sidewalk, but few turn to look.

We make our way to the National Gallery, and I see Trafalgar Square for the first time. I can't get over it. Pigeons clamour over tourists. Millions of birds chase after bread crumbs. A towering monument, guarded by four enormous lions, points to the sky. "Who's the guy at the top?" Donna asks. But I don't know. "Wellington," someone says, tapping me on the shoulder. "Defeated Napoleon, he did. We'd all be speaking French, if he hadn't." On the far side of the square stands Canada House. I see a Canadian flag and salute. Donna howls.

"Go chase some pigeons," she says. She pulls her camera out and tells me to run into the flock. But before I can move a bird hops onto my shoulder.

Click! Click!

Donna's caught that one.

"Now run," she says. And I do. I dash into a crowd of pigeons and the birds rush into the air in a flurry of flapping wings. But they don't go far, and they're soon replaced.

Then Donna commands me to lie down. "On the ground. Face up." And as I follow out her command, she buys some birdseed from a vendor, which she sprinkles across me, head to foot. Quickly, I'm covered in pigeons, poking at my clothes, digging their pointy toes into my chest and arms.

Click! Click!

Donna's recorded everything.

I roll over and pull myself up on one knee just before a pigeon jumps onto my face. Donna grins and brushes birdseed out of my hair.

"Thanks, Daniel," she says.

I stand up and hug her. She buries her face in my neck. The world disappears.

Later, we meet Peter.

We are on our way to St. John's Wood to pick up Donna's things, when we see him on the other side of the street in the company of two young men. Americans, it turns out. John Kennedy and George Washington. Two presidents reincarnated. Donna waves to them, but they don't see us. As we get closer, we realize that the Americans are supporting Peter, holding him up by his elbows. All three are stone drunk.

Peter sees us first. He looks up, then lurches into the street, calling Donna's name.

"My god," I say, as an approaching car slams on its brakes, narrowly missing Peter.

Peter waves at the driver, who is laying on his horn.

"Donna, Donna," he says, staggering towards her.

Then he throws his arms around her and plants a kiss on her cheek. John and George follow behind him, holding hands. Donna pushes herself away from Peter and says, "Come, we better get you home." She turns him around and leads him in the direction he came from.

I assume that John and George are the friends Peter is staying with, but they laugh at the suggestion. They are Peter's neighbours, they say. Their parents, all four sets of them—"One of the benefits of divorce is that the bowl is that much deeper"—have rented a house for the pair in London for the year. "To see how we like it, you know. Living together and all." They were Harvard students who fell in love. "But life is too short to spend your best years in school, don't you think?"

Donna and Peter lead the way, his arm draped over her shoulders. I try to start a conversation with John and

George, but they are full of inside jokes. Everything I say produces a comment and a snicker, and soon we are walking in silence, John and George trading glances, Peter whispering in Donna's ear.

The house where Peter is staying turns out to be substantially larger than I had imagined. A willow tree fills the front yard. A colourful garden brightens the front of the house. Peter unlocks the door and ushers us in. The hardwood floor appears freshly polished. The walls are decorated with paintings. John and George disappear into the kitchen. Peter directs me into the front room, then remains in the hall with Donna. I interest myself in the books that line three of the walls and find leather-bound first editions of Dickens and Austen. Something's happening here, but I don't know what. John and George appear with a decanter of whiskey and a bucket of ice.

"Have they gone upstairs?" George asks.

"You know they have," says John, dumping ice into three glasses and pouring the whiskey. Then he turns to me. "You're going to lose that girl," he says in a mock–serious tone, and stops pouring suddenly, realizing what he's said. "That's a Beatles line, isn't it?" He looks at me, but when I don't respond, he glances at George for confirmation. "You know." He sings, "'You're going to lose that girl, yes, yes, you're going to lose that girl. You're going to loo-oo-oose that, lose that girl.' Oh, forget it."

George laughs. For some reason, he finds this hilariously funny. He holds his sides and chuckles, but he can't hold it in, and he's soon leaning back in his chair, overcome by giggles.

"What's the matter with you?" John says, but he can hardly keep himself from laughing, too. "This is a serious moment. A tragedy is brewing." He turns to me and again adopts his mock-serious tone. "Young man, it is necessary that we discuss certain particulars." But he can't maintain his posture. He attempts a sip of whiskey, but he laughs and coughs it back up.

"Step back a moment in your mind's eye," he advises me. "A young couple, a pair of queers, a third gentleman. Consider the possibilities. No, wait. Consider the point of view of the queers. Hell, George," he turns to his partner. "We should just tell him. The dramatic irony is killing me."

George puts his hand on his chin and adopts a pose of intense listening. "Right you are," he says eventually. "But have you considered the consequences? He may be a raving lunatic inside that calm exterior. The serial murderer type, John. Have you factored my safety into your moral responsibility?"

"Bullocks," says John. "Let's ask him, shall we?"

"Right," says George, addressing me. "Are you the serial killer type, then?"

"No," I say.

"Good," says George. And I suddenly realize that they're talking in English accents.

But before they can tell me any more, Donna emerges from the doorway, bag in hand.

"I've got my stuff, Daniel," she says. She surveys the room and the smirks embedded on the faces of my companions.

"Nice meeting you two," she says as I pass her and head for the door.

"Double your pleasure," I hear John say. "I don't know why I said that." Then there is a burst of giggles, and Donna pushes me down the stairs and along the front walk. We're halfway across the street before she says anything.

"Do you know what he said to me?"

I confess ignorance.

"He said that he was in love with me. Grand, isn't it? Isn't that fucking grand." Then she waits for me to say something, but I don't, and she lets out a deep sigh, and turns away from me.

"I'm sure you don't understand any of this," she says.

"You're right," I say. And suddenly I realize we're standing in front of the Beatles's Abbey Road studios and I'm staring at the crosswalk that graces the cover of the group's last studio album. I stop and point. "We're here." And Donna looks, too. She lowers her pack off her shoulder and digs for her camera.

"Take your shoes and socks off and walk across," she says. "Like Paul did." But I don't. I just stand and stare at the crosswalk. White lines painted in foot wide bands spread across the road. I can hardly make sense of it. Nothing holds together. And I'm a long way from home.

PARENTS

Richard disappeared ten days after Sandi told him she was pregnant. He rose for school, ate breakfast, vanished. Six months later, he turned up in British Columbia, held in a Vancouver jail, arrested with a group of activists for blocking a logging road. His father flew out to pay the bail and bring him home. Richard disappeared again two days later.

Damn you, Richard. Sandi wishes she had never met him. Damn you, Mr. Hit and Run. She feels the baby growing inside her. Her friends ask to feel her belly. Two of them have told her they envy her. Her father tells her not to worry. Worry? Why should she worry? Babies are beautiful. Babies are the best.

She was the new girl at school. A Maritime lass alone in the city. Her parents divorced, and she followed her father to Toronto. It was raining the day she met Richard. Late September, Back to School Dance. Richard kept calling—and she has to admit she loved it; she swam in the attention. He called, and they talked into the morning hours. He told her about his parents. He told her about his friends. He was eager for his life to begin, he said. She said, Why don't you come over? She thought that it would last forever, run like a river, roar like Niagara, but the wave crashed and retreated, his first time.

Richard hates his name. It's his father's name. His friends used to call him Richie, until he punched three of them out. He was twelve or thirteen, he said. He told Sandi he couldn't remember how old he was, but he remembered people stopped calling him Richie after that.

Sandi has it figured out. Richard shares his parents' values, she tells her diary. Richard's greatest fear is to be thought different from his peers; his peers rally behind the slogan, Parents Suck. It's a violent circle, a cruelty she has learned to accept. Sandi has the goods on Richard's parents. His father met his mother on a cruise to Bermuda. This was in the Sixties. The cruise was a graduation present. Richard's father was on his way to law school. Richard's mother was an art student, working her way through college. She moved in with her future husband later that year. They rented an apartment on Spadina north of Bloor and stayed there until Richard's father entered the law firm established by his grandfather fifty years earlier. They moved to Don Mills, then. Richard's mother loved the freshness she felt in the broad streets, the ordered lawns. As a hobby, Richard's father bought and sold old cars. He has the emotional maturity of a Mack truck, Sandi tells her diary. He spends his weekends fixing cars he never drives, his head sunk into the motor of a Ford or a Chevrolet, the radio on, his house not ten metres but a universe away. Sandi can't stand the man, which, she figures, helps to explain Pedro, the part-time model and exotic dancer Richard's mother met at a charity dinner. That's the story Sandi heard, anyway. Richard's mother took her to coffee after Richard disappeared. *We should talk*, Richard's mother said. *I want you to think of me as your friend*. Richard's mother told Sandi that Pedro was a terrific lover. *Like in the movies*, she said. Richard's mother said she couldn't believe she was going to be a granny. *It's so exciting*, she said.

Richard returns after the baby's born and tells Sandi they should get back together. *We were good together*, he says. The baby is asleep. Her father is out. Sandi thought it would be good to see Richard. Talking is good, she figured. He is the father, after all, but she's less sure of that all the time. He may have contributed half of her baby's genetic code, but he ain't no father. *I don't want to sleep with you, Richard*, she says. *You lost that privilege*. She wants to tell him about the birth. About the six hours of labour and the nurse who asked about her husband. Was he going to join her in the delivery room? Her father was out of town on business. Her mother had advised her to get an abortion. But she doesn't tell him any of these things. She just says, *I think it's time for you to go*, and he does.

PARKED CARS

"Get lost, kid," the man said.

"Come on, man."

Jimmy looked at the man and stuck his thumb in the back pocket of his jeans. I felt like running.

"Just give us one," he said.

The man didn't move. He turned and looked down the beach. It was hard to stand there. I watched the other people walking past. I watched a dog catch a frisbee and a baby crawling in the grass.

"Why should I?" the man said.

Jimmy had him now, but I didn't want to wait. I didn't care. This wasn't my game. I thought about last night. I thought about my mother yelling at me.

"Because," Jimmy said.

The man had a black t-shirt and a tear in his jeans. He had long hair and a moustache.

"Just because," Jimmy said. "So we'll leave you alone."

The man looked at me and I knew he could tell I wasn't in this, but I was. I looked at him to tell him I was in it. I looked at his face, then I looked at his shoulder. He had a tattoo. I couldn't see what it was. It was under his t-shirt, but I could see that he had one.

Jimmy said he was going to get a tattoo, too. He said that a month ago, but he still didn't have one.

The man pulled a cigarette out from behind his ear and handed it to Jimmy.

"Now get lost," he said.

"It's illegal to give a cigarette to a minor," said Jimmy, and we ran. We ran down the boardwalk and didn't turn around. I thought he was after us at first, but then I realized he wasn't. We ran all the way to the rocks. We climbed over them and hid in our favourite cave. It was almost too small for us now. It was better when we were little.

Jimmy pulled out his lighter and lit the cigarette. He took a couple of drags and handed it to me. I didn't like smoking, but I did it anyway. I didn't want to get addicted. Jimmy said he was addicted. That was why he bummed cigarettes. He started when he was nine and he couldn't stop. I smoked with Jimmy because he was my friend. I didn't do it much. I didn't want to get cancer like my grandfather. He got cancer from smoking and he said if he ever heard anything about me smoking he would make me regret it. I didn't want to die like him. I was going to die someday. I knew that. But I didn't want to get cancer. Your body goes crazy on you. It turns against you, my grandfather said, because it knows smoking is bad for you, but if you do it anyway then it gets you later. I didn't want that to happen.

I heard if you froze to death it was like sleeping. You got a warm feeling and you didn't even know you were dying. You're freezing to death and you feel warm. That's how I want to die.

Jimmy asked me what I was thinking about. He always said I thought too much, which is probably true. Jimmy thinks a lot, too, but not like me. I think about stuff and Jimmy does stuff. That's why we're friends.

"I was thinking about last night," I said. I didn't want to tell him I was thinking about death. The cigarette was almost gone now.

"What about it?" he said.

"I don't know," I said. "It was cool, I guess."

Jimmy nodded and crushed out the cigarette on a rock. He knew I got in shit for staying out late. He didn't have a curfew. At least, he said he didn't. My mother grounded me for a week, but today was Saturday. You couldn't ground anyone on a Saturday. Next week I had to go straight home from school and do my homework and read books. No TV. No movies. No computer games. It sucked, but it was worth it.

Last night we went to the park. After it got dark we crawled down the hill into the valley and watched the parked cars. We crawled right up behind this parked car and watched two people going at it. Right there in the car. You could see them kissing. Then they fell down out of sight and the car started to shake. Jimmy started laughing. I couldn't believe it. I thought we were going to get killed, but they didn't hear us. Jimmy had a hard-on after that. He said he did, anyway. He wanted me to feel it, but I said he was crazy.

THE LOWEST BRANCH

"He got himself up there and then he didn't know what to do with himself."

My father says this and takes a drag on his cigarette. He's sitting in the middle of our backyard in a lawn chair. It's Wednesday afternoon and he should be at work, but I got stuck up a tree in the park near our house, and my mother called him and asked him to come home and get me down.

"Your mother thinks that I'm the goddamn fire department," he said as he stood at the bottom of the ladder and leaned it against the lowest branch of the tree. I was twenty feet off the ground, looking down at him.

"What were you doing up there?"

I didn't say anything.

We didn't say anything to each other on the way home, either. He carried the ladder and smoked a cigarette, and I walked beside him in the gutter, kicking stones. Half an hour later my mother called me out of my room and said my father wanted to see me in the backyard.

He rested his beer bottle against his knee.

"Danny," he said, "what were you doing up that tree?"
I said I didn't know.
"You must have been doing something."
I shook my head.
"Nothing, you say."
I didn't move.
"Nothing at all?"
"No."
He slapped his free hand against his leg.
"He got himself up there and then he didn't know what to do with himself," he said and dragged on his cigarette. "Can you imagine that."
I stared at my shoes. I wanted to go back to my room. I didn't want to be standing there. I crossed my feet and stepped on my right foot. I uncrossed them and stepped on my left.
"Do you know where I should be right now, Danny?"
I knew, but I didn't want to say.
My father waited about half an hour and then he said, "Do you know, Danny?"
I still hadn't uncrossed my feet. I could feel the big toe on my left foot turning purple.
"Yes," I said.
"And where's that?" he said.
"At work," I said.
"At work," he said. "Very good."
I could feel the back of my neck turning red. The sun was hot on my neck, but that wasn't why it was red. I was still looking at my shoes. I uncrossed my feet and looked at him. I never asked my mother to call him. I never did. I would have come down. I didn't need him to get me down. I don't know why she called him. I could have done it.
"Do you know why I go to work, Danny?"
I sat down on the grass and pulled my knees to my chest.
"Stand up," he said. He almost yelled it. "Stand on your damn feet and talk to me like a man." He was yelling now. He leaned forward in his chair and grabbed me by the elbow.

He shook me and I fell sideways onto the grass. I didn't move, but he stayed in his chair.

I watched him. He took a drink from his beer and stubbed out his cigarette. "Why do I go to work, Danny?" he said.

"To make money."

"To make money. Very good."

I rolled over on the grass and sat up with my legs crossed. I knew that I was going to say it, but I didn't want to say it. I thought about not saying it. I never asked her to call him. Why should I say it? I thought about not saying it. I thought about telling him why I was up the tree. I always go up that tree. I go up there because my mother thinks I can't get down. She didn't have to call him.

"I'm sorry," I said.

"Thank you, Danny," he said.

I rolled over and watched an ant crawl through the grass.

DREW BARRYMORE'S BREASTS

I was watching television with my mother the night Drew Barrymore flashed David Letterman. I don't know if you saw this. Drew jumped up on Dave's desk, danced around for a few seconds, then lifted her t-shirt and showed Dave her breasts. After she returned to her seat, Dave said, "You don't know how much I thank you for that."

Drew laughed. Later she would tell Dave that she had multiple personality disorder, so it wasn't necessary for her to create characters when she acted. All she had to do was call up one of her personalities.

My mother fell asleep before Drew showed Dave her breasts, but when I woke her up to guide her to her room, she saw one of the many times the producers replayed it.

"What was that all about?" she asked.

"Nothing," I said.

It was late. I led her to her bedroom and kissed her on the cheek.

"Good night," I said. "Sweet dreams."

I pulled the door shut and walked down the hallway to my room. All the lights were out in the house except the one in the front room, where we had the television. I could walk around this house for a week blindfolded and not bump into anything. I have lived here my whole life.

I walked into my room and took a bottle of whiskey out of the top drawer of my dresser. I have a Led Zepplin poster over my bed. It has been there since I was fifteen. I was thinking about taking it down, since I just graduated from college.

I took the whiskey into the kitchen. My mother didn't like to see me drinking. My father had stopped drinking two years ago because he was an alcoholic. My mother didn't like to see me drinking, but she didn't stop me. I took some ice cubes out of the freezer and dropped them in a glass.

I took the whiskey and the glass full of ice cubes with me to the front room. Letterman was still on. I picked up the remote control and pressed "stop" on the VCR. The machine clicked, then whirled when I pressed "rewind." I wanted to watch Drew Barrymore again.

She jumps up on his desk and you can tell by the look on his face that he's thinking, *Oh, boy. What now?* The interview is out of his control. Then she lifts up her shirt. You can't see anything. Maybe the side of her breast. Just a shadow. She's facing Dave and he's staring up at her breasts. For maybe half a second he's sitting there staring up at her breasts. He can definitely see both of her nipples. The camera shows you Dave under Drew's right elbow and his eyes are hanging out of his face.

Drew jumps off the desk and sits down. She's nervous about what he's going to say, you can tell. She took control of the interview, but then she gave it back. She sits there looking like a nervous schoolgirl, nibbling on her fingernails. But Dave thanks her and she laughs. She's relieved. You can tell she's thinking, *It was good. I didn't ruin the interview.* The audience is screaming and clapping and the producers replay it over and over.

My mother looked at it and shook her head. She never used to watch Letterman. My father died two months ago. My poor mother. She's not very well.

She works at the local library. They gave her a leave of absence when my father died, but she hasn't gone back.

"They don't need me," she said when I asked her about it.

But you need them, I thought. She had hardly been outside since she put my father in the ground. I didn't push her, though. You don't get anywhere by pushing people, I can tell you that.

I took a sip of whiskey. It burned the back of my throat. Dave was saying to the audience, "I'm at work here! You people come here for entertainment, but this is my job!" He made his eyes go big and took a drink from his mug.

"This is my job!" he said again, and they replayed Drew lifting up her shirt.

My father drove a taxi, okay. He was killed when a passenger demanded his money. He turned over the money, and the passenger shot him in the back of the head. My mother cried all the way through the funeral. The church was packed with taxi drivers from as far away as Ottawa and Montreal. Death can bring people together, I guess.

I stopped the VCR and began flipping through the channels. I stopped on an old episode of "Three's Company," then flipped to a conversation two old guys were having about the work of the Devil.

FLYING TRUCK WHEELS

I'm stocking shelves at the supermarket when an old woman passes me. "Oh my," she says. Then she falls, collapses, dead at my feet.

I try to tell my mother about it, but she just sips her gin and tonic. It's my father's weekend to take me.

After my father picks me up, I tell him Jimmy Harding wants to fuck me. We're weird that way, me and my dad. We talk about things that I could never talk about with my mom. Like boys. I don't think she knows so much about that, anyway. She and my dad are split up, I mean. That says something.

Jimmy Harding wants to fuck me, I tell my dad, and he doesn't say anything. We're on the Parkway, heading north. My dad's got a place up there, a cottage. It belongs to his family, really. My family, too. My three uncles and one aunt, but not my two other aunts, my mother's sisters. They don't have a cottage. Only houses, families, husbands, kids. My father has a cottage, and we like to go there. In the summer we swim and water ski. In the winter I used to build snow forts. Now we ice–fish sometimes, or I just read books.

My dad knows Jimmy Harding. Knows about him, anyway. I talk about him a lot. We're pals. He got me my job at the supermarket. He can get booze when we want it. He's got a great CD collection, and I've kissed him a couple of times. We tried going out last summer, like boyfriend and girlfriend, but it was really stupid. After a week he tried to boss me around, and that was end of that. Then he started going out with this other girl, Jennifer. She's got big tits, which made me jealous for a while, but my father talked me out of that. Thank God.

"So what do you think, Dad?"

He's an introvert, my father. Introfuckingverted.

Hello.

Then he says what I knew he would say. He asks me how I feel about it.

I don't want to fuck Jimmy Harding. Let's be clear about that right now. But there's a couple of things going on here that I want to explore. First, if I don't fuck Jimmy Harding, what happens to our friendship? Or if I do, same question. Second. Talking to my dad like this is a test for the real thing. What happens when I meet someone whom I want to fuck, I mean. So you can agree with me that the best thing is to not let on. To everything, turn, turn, turn, and all that. Jimmy taught me to play poker, so I know how to bluff. An iceberg is nine-tenths under water.

My dad asks me how I feel about the fact that Jimmy Harding wants to fuck me, and I tell him, I don't know, you know, I thought maybe I would just blow him.

I say crazy things like that sometimes for no reason.

Blow him. Blow the man down.

My dad goes back to the silent treatment. He knows I can be funny. Say things for no reason like I just did. He's got patience for that. Much more than my mother.

My mother doesn't like my jokes.

My mother rides me when I free–associate, say stupid things, or try to have a good time. I like to play with words, but my mother has a fragile sense of reality. Her imagination frightens her, is what I mean. Not my dad, though. He's different. According to my mother, the world is one way and only one way. My mother can't stack words. That's what I call it when I make things up. It's not lying. I'm not lying. It's not deceit. You believe me, right? It's fun. My mother can't dance, and she doesn't read books. She can't stack words, and she can't take a joke.

I tell my dad I think I'm ready for sex, but I'm unsure if I want to have sex with Jimmy Harding.

Then it sounds like you're not ready for sex, he says.

He says: You'll know you're ready when you're ready.

Which is another thing he always says.

I decide to drop this conversation. We're ripping down the highway. We pass an old barn, the wooden walls worn grey from decades of rain and winter. When I see things like that, I wish I lived in the country. I like the way old barns look when they're all alone in a field, half falling down, surrounded by flowers and wild grass.

Ten minutes later we stop for gas and a burger. I get out of the car and leave my dad standing at the pump. I walk over to the snack bar beside the gas station. I buy a pack of gum. I get a lonely feeling standing at the counter, waiting for my change. I don't know why. I think it's because I grew up in the city. The snack bar is beside the gas station which is beside the highway which goes back and forth to the city or, if you go in the other direction, north to somewhere that I don't know, to my father's cottage and beyond. What I'm saying is, the snack bar is nowhere. Feels like it's nowhere. It's close to the pretty barn, but it's not pretty. Sometimes I try to think about what it would be like to live in different places around the world. If I tried that with this snack bar, I think I would freak out.

I look for my dad and see he's already found a table at the burger joint beside the snack bar beside the gas station.

I'm fifteen, but I only met my dad three years ago. He used to live in Vancouver, but now he lives in Etobicoke, which is at the other end of the city from where I live, but only about an hour away if the traffic isn't bad.

I live with my mother. Every other weekend I live with my father. Sometimes when I'm mad at my mother I run away to my father's. This pisses my mother off. She says it "undermines" her "authority," but my father doesn't make me go back. He lets me do what I want, more or less. The problem is, all my friends live in the east end, and if I want to be near them, then I need to be at my mother's. Plus, living with my mother isn't all bad. Sometimes she buys me stuff. A radio, or a dress, or tickets to a concert or a show. She likes to take me to the theatre, and I think that's great.

My father does something in an office. I don't know what. He wears a suit and a tie and slicks his hair back and looks real smart. He's losing his hair, but when he slicks it back you don't notice. He carries a briefcase and a cellular phone. He does lunch with people. Once I did lunch with him. I met him downtown and we did lunch. That was right after he came back. I was twelve and I giggled a lot. It was the first time that I had a father, a real father. My mother had a boyfriend, but he didn't live with us, and we never tried to pretend he was my father. We went to a movie once, me and my mother's boyfriend. My mother wanted us to. And it was okay. He bought me a large popcorn. Later my mother said he didn't like kids.

My father orders a burger, and I order a burger and fries. One of my friends at school is a vegetarian, and she wants me to become a vegetarian, too. But so far, no. I almost did about a year ago, but then my friend stopped being a vegetarian for a month, and I didn't want to be one on my own.

I ask my father about Linda. Linda's his girlfriend. They used to live together, but now they don't. They broke up, then they got back together, but they don't live together. I like Linda, but my father says she doesn't know what she wants. One time I asked Linda what she wanted. I was over at my father's, and he was out buying groceries or something. It was after they had broken up and gotten back together. She moved out, and this was a couple of months after that. We were watching TV, and Linda was asking me about my future, if I thought about university, and what I wanted to do with my life. I don't know, I said. *What about you? What do you want?* She said that she just wanted to be happy. I told my father that, and he wanted to know if I asked her what would make her happy. No, I said. I was saving that for next time.

We spend about three-quarters of an hour eating. My father orders a coffee, and I get an ice cream. Then we get back on the road. Before we're out of the parking lot, I slam a Rolling Stones tape in the deck. My mother listens to a lot of hippie music, and sometimes I do, too.

II

For years, the girl, his daughter, had been a hole in his life, a silence, the unfortunate consequence of a hurried coupling, a void that had grown with an organic consistency, swallowing the what-might-have-beens, alternate histories, memories of distant dreams, hopes, futures, until the day his mother died, and the sky opened, and the world shook, and his grief roared out of him like an animal from the lower reaches of the underworld. What had he made of himself? Who was he? He requested a transfer. He began to settle his affairs. The company packed him off to Toronto, and it was only then he remembered his daughter. Ten times the planet had spun around the sun, travelling thousands of millions of miles through an empty universe, since he had seen her, and somewhere in the folds of space and time she had disappeared, misplaced in his memory until his soul shuddered and groaned under what friends dismissed as a

73

mid-life crisis and which he knew to be something more. He consulted his lawyer, freed funds for support payments, hardened his heart against her mother, the woman he had once loved furtively, selectively, selfishly, and whom he now found he resented as an obstacle to his healing.

In his childhood, he had dreamed of no more than asserting himself. Finding his place. Making it. He had attached no image to that desire, and found in the midst of his crisis no memory to ground him, only a feeling that pulsed through his veins and cried for relief, a vague, all–encompassing fear that his life was ending without beginning. He had all that he knew how to acquire—and also nothing.

So went his thoughts one morning, a Saturday, as he lay in bed, his nostrils full of the scent of the prostitute he had dismissed in a fit of pique, a sudden need to be alone. It was the morning of the day he would meet her, his daughter. He turned into his pillow. Crushed it against his face. His mind flooded with scenes from his imagined future, and he felt a pulsing behind his temples; his life thundered around him like a mid-summer storm, rolling in from the west, displacing the stagnant city air, and he felt caught in a powerful wind which lifted him off the ground and shot him through glittering corridors, across great plains, over disparate, dazzling geographies that rushed beneath him as he planed over their surfaces like a low–flying aircraft, an eagle or a cruise missile. Arrangements had been made. Deals struck. His daughter would meet him. They had spoken on the phone, her voice clear as a bouquet of roses.

They met at a downtown hotel. She appeared, an apparition turned inward, all emotion withdrawn, a shy, halting, huddled figure of a girl, copied cell by cell (it seemed to him) from her mother. They shook hands, and he led her to the elevator and a restaurant overlooking the city. She warmed to him slowly, and he played hard to get, gingerly winning her trust. They spent the afternoon at the museum, staring up at the dinosaurs, admiring the mediaeval armour. Then he packed her into a taxi. Sent her home. Took himself to a movie and sat in the darkness, crying out his happiness.

Three months later, as their visits multiplied, his enthusiasm for their relationship continued unabated, reaching new heights with each encounter. He took her up the CN Tower, to the Home and Garden Show, to rock concerts, to the symphony, book launches, hockey games, on weekend trips to New York City, Montréal, Paris, filling her with the best of everything he knew and everything that he knew to be the best. And his soul pounded with gratitude. Had he ever been more content, more sure of his place in the world? He sought and achieved a promotion, moved into a new condo on the lakefront, played the market with more daring, picking stocks over his breakfast toast and tea. Through a client, he met Linda, an aspiring twenty-three-year-old with a warm bosom and sharp legs. She cradled his head in her arms the first time they made love, rode the wave of his confidence, gushing his praises to friends wary of their age difference; he bought her diamonds, a sports car, rare books and roses. She admired how he insisted his daughter came first, marvelled how the girl and the man complemented each other, their joy palpable at every meeting.

One weekend in early fall, the trees easing into their new uniforms, the girl's father invited his lover and daughter to overnight with him in Niagara Falls. Down the highway the three sped, listening to one of the girl's favourite cassettes, then tucked themselves into a lavish hotel overlooking Horseshoe Falls and its continual rich thunder. They stood on their balcony stupefied by the volume of water, and he thought simply about their insignificance as individuals in nature's rage against permanence. It was a moment none of them would understand, though it was a sort of apex, a point in time that would alter the balance of their lives. They walked the promenade, bought hot dogs and ice cream, visited the waxworks museum, slipped exuberantly into the role of tourists, and revelled in the tackiness and commercialism others had constructed around one of the natural world's true wonders. The man swelled with pleasure as his daughter held Linda's hand and giggled at a shared witticism. That night, he held his lover close and felt complete, confident finally that every gear had found its groove, every planet its orbit, and he fell asleep into a pit of absolute darkness.

In the weeks that followed, the man glided blindly into a new weather system, minimizing Linda's mild concerns, then cautions, then complaints about his distance from her needs. They had a good thing going, then they didn't. What happened? She wanted to live with him; he said no. She told him of her lonely nights, her hunger for him, her mounting jealousy of his daughter, her anxieties that she was the cause of the end of their joy. Weepy phone calls evolved into blunt accusations, pointed words, frigid nights, anxiety, anger, depression, and eventual reconciliation. He invited her to move in. He apologized. Together they promised a return to the glow of their early days. They spoke of restoration, renewal, regeneration, acknowledging an inarticulated loss, weaving a patch for an unlabelled wound. And for six months their hope held. For six months the architecture of their relationship channelled their lives along parallel paths, joining their hearts in harmony, fulfilling the rhythms of their bodies. For six months, their work, their play, their love of each other and the girl rolled into an aesthetic whole, filling their lonely moments with colour, relieving their anxieties with a promise of relief, the blessing of continual pleasure. Then Linda moved out. She didn't know what she wanted. She felt smothered. They separated without enmity, but the girl was devastated, the gas tank of her lyricism suddenly drained. Sometimes people get too close, her father attempted to explain to her, no longer sure himself of the sequence of events or their meaning. What had happened?

A year later, he still didn't know. The wave crested and broke; the undertow pulled them back below the surface, submerged them in their anxieties, then threw them back toward the shore. His future had come to him as a flood, lifting him out of the blankness of his past, but the rising waters had also changed the geography of his life, releasing new turbulence, challenging him with new unknowns, new uncertainties. A year after Linda walked out, they continued to see each other, continued to love each other, continued to seek the path back to the greater good, the sugar of their first months together, but he came slowly to realize that what he had originally experienced as loss, he now felt to be a gain. A new awareness of the world. *Why do we expect to be understood? Why do we expect our desires to be fulfilled?* The mysteries of the world are of a different order. This was a conclusion that locked him more deeply to his life than ever, and it released him from anxieties about the drifts of his relationship to Linda, opened his eyes to new possibilities, opened his ears to new rhythms, new harmonies. He began to see his daughter, for example, for the curious person she was, a teenager negotiating with grace the struggles of adolescence, and he came to marvel at her changes, her curiosity, her intelligence. He enjoyed listening to her, hearing about her friends, encouraging her tentative exploration of her sexuality, providing her with information about the larger world, the world of money, the world of sex, the world of disappointment. One weekend he arranged to take her to the cottage, one of their favourite places. He picked her up from her mother's house and listened to her stories as they sped along the highway, stopping briefly at a roadside diner for lunch before continuing on their way.

III

"Happy birthday, Cheryl. How many candles?"

"Seventeen."

The man settles into a seat at the counter, third from the right, unbuttons his denim jacket and pulls an Expos cap off his head. On the far side of the highway diner, two elderly women in cotton jackets smoke unfiltered cigarettes and swap photographs of their grandchildren. In the booth beside them, three teenagers pick through soggy French fries and smear ketchup on the table with their fingers. The youngest picks up a glass, drains the last mouthful of pop, spits into the remaining ice. The old women laugh at a shared memory, the pale echo of their joy drifting into a rumble of thunder. The man pushes his hair back over his head, bending it around his ears. Water runs cool down his neck, soaking into the collar of his dusty work shirt. Outside, a heavy rain pounds the glass walls, drumming nature's beat.

The waitress glances at the clock, bites the inside of her cheek. Her shift is over, her replacement fifteen minutes late. Six months ago she quit school. Her boyfriend has been fucking one of her friends. She rings the man's money into the till, feels his eyes tracing the outline of her uniform.

"Brutal weather," she says.

"You bet."

"That's bad for business."

Last week, they talked about why people did things; why certain events happened; the sadness she feels whenever she turns on the news. He told her about his younger brother, the murderer, who was about to be released from fifteen years in prison.

She stands opposite him, her back against the wall, her arms hanging loose at her sides. She wants to ask him about the car accident that killed a man and his daughter. A flying truck wheel crashed through the windshield of their car, crushing them, smashing the girl's skull like a Hallowe'en pumpkin. Others have told her he was the first to the scene. She cut the girl's picture out of the newspaper and taped it to the wall above her bed. The girl was a year younger than her. She tries to imagine the girl's life. What did she wear? like? dance to? She feels the girl died to tell her something. Something remains of her. She has felt something in the air.

The man lays his left hand on the counter, palm down, and spreads out his fingers. His nails are short and dirty, his skin dry, battered. The man fixes farm machinery for money, plays hockey or softball, depending on the season. Stories of teammates, neighbours, wives and girlfriends of teammates and neighbours fill his visits to the diner. She listens, constructing in her mind a vision of his world. One of the teenagers across the room calls to her.

"How about a coffee here? Could we have some coffee here?"

The man lifts the edge of a bandage off his palm, pulls it up a quarter-inch, then pushes it down with his thumb, flattening it like a postage stamp.

She steps to her left to fill a cup of coffee for the teenager, glances at the door, hoping to see her replacement. Snake lines of rain shine on the windows in the neon light of the diner. A sliver of lightning sparks across the sky, streaking through the storm behind the trees on the far side of the highway. The waitress delivers the teenager his coffee, asks the elderly women if she can get them anything. The women order more coffee. One of them takes a hold of her sleeve. Is today her birthday? She couldn't help but overhear the man ask her about it. Is today the day?

"No," the waitress says. "Yesterday."

The woman asks her what she did to celebrate.

"I had a party," she says, telling the woman what she is sure she wants to hear, though the truth is something else. The truth is, she spent the evening on the phone, trying to hunt down her boyfriend. They had planned to spend the evening together, but he never arrived. Her parents were in

Toronto on business. She waited in front of the TV, flipping between music videos, European soccer and a talk show. She took one of her father's beers out of the fridge, called her boyfriend's parents. He's on his way, they said. But an hour later, he still hadn't arrived. She called his best friend, she called his sister, she called his hockey coach, she waited another hour, then she called the girl she knew he was fucking. No one answered. She opened another beer and searched for her mother's cigarettes. It was less than twenty-four hours since she had taken him in the back seat of his pickup in the parking lot behind the arena. Less than twenty-four hours since she had tried to suck the blood out of his face, tearing at his lips with her teeth, throwing herself on his cock. She burned for him as much as she hated him. She wondered if the dead girl had a boyfriend. She sat in her room, cross-legged on her bed, surrounded by candles, and thought about the dead girl. She closed her eyes and tried to remember the dead girl's face.

"I had a party," she tells the old woman. "All my friends came. We had a big cake, and we played music, and we danced."

The woman is smiling at her, and she smiles back.

"Sounds like you had a good time," the other woman says.

The waitress nods and pulls a cloth from a pocket in her apron, wipes a stain off their table.

It was her boyfriend's little brother who told her what she already suspected. The fourteen-year-old had a pure heart, and she knew he had betrayed his brother because he refused to harbour deceit. Her boyfriend, she knew, professed loyalty not to her, but to himself; his commitment wasn't to her, but to the demands of his personality, his psyche, the previously established pattern of his existence. His balls. His chaos was a constant she depended upon, a storm which delighted her soul, took her into herself as she fought to repair the damage and dance through each day, hungry for a deeper connection with the world.

The man scratches the stubble on his cheek, lights his cigarette. She notes a scar above his left eye, a red mark about an inch long which protrudes delicately from his scalp. It's a mark that's new to her, something she knows nothing about.

"You saw that accident," she says.

He looks up at her.

"Didn't see it. Heard it."

He reaches for an ashtray, waits to see if she wants to know more.

She crosses her ankles and, lacing her fingers together in front of her, leans her back against the wall. Thunder shakes the diner. She feels a wave of heat race up her legs and along her spine. The sensation shoots up her vertebrae and disperses across her shoulders before sliding down her arms to her palms, where it forms into a ball. When she pushes her palms together, the ball rolls around her wrists, first her left then her right, where it floats for a few seconds before drifting to her waist and up towards her breasts. It enters her body below her ribs, and she feels flush with life, her blood roaring with approval.

"It was a bad news scene," the man continues his story, knocking the ashes off his smoke.

The waitress stares into his eyes.

"I walked out of the house," he says. "I was thinking how beautiful the day had been, when suddenly there was a giant squeal of tires and a crash. I couldn't see anything at first, but then I saw the truck roll to a stop on the shoulder. I didn't see the car until I got up to the road."

Gerry's Sister
(Mercy in the Night)

A month before her wedding, my sister calls me at three o'clock in the morning and says she's told her fiancé the thing she had promised me she would never tell him.

I ask her, Why did you do that?

He needed to know, Gerry, she says.

Maybe he did, I say, and maybe he didn't.

I can hear her crying on the other end of the line.

I ask her what happened. She says they were in bed, and he asked her if she had any secrets. We can't have any secrets from each other, he said, and so she told him, and he just sat there for a minute, then he got dressed and left.

I ask her if he said anything.

No, she says. I don't know. No. Maybe. Oh, Gerry. What am I going to do?

Just sit there, I tell her. I can hear her sobbing. I promise her I'll be there as soon as I can. I have a girl in bed with me. I have her half undressed, and she has her hand on the inside of my leg, but I tell her the night's over. I tell her I'll take her home. I gotta go see my sister. She's a Chinese girl.

Young. Pretty. She rubs the inside of my leg, and I stick my finger inside her.

My sister's twenty-four, and she works in a hairstyling place. Her fiancé is thirty, and he works in a bank. They met on the internet. I bought my sister a computer three years ago and got her hooked up to the Web, and within a week or two she started spending hours hanging out in chat rooms, meeting people. She said she liked it because you could get intimate with people real quick, and you could dump them fast, too, if they turned you off. My sister has that gift. I don't. She can ask someone the most startling question within the first minute of meeting them. "Do you think that masturbation is a healthy expression of self-esteem, or the opposite?" "Pornography is a powerful stimulant, don't you think?" It might surprise you to know how many people appreciate the direct approach. The others she wins over with her laughter. She is an attractive woman, my sister, eminently likeable and adored by all.

I take the Chinese girl back downtown, then drive north on Bathurst. I make sure to get the Chinese girl's phone number. Her name's Denise. I promise I'll call soon. She's a social work student, but she thinks she might want to be a nurse. She enjoys helping people. My sister has an apartment north of St. Clair, near where Hemingway lived in the 1920s.

At Bloor Street, my cell phone rings. I'm sitting at the light, reading the slogans on the side of Honest Ed's, wondering how he gets away with all those bulbs. I pick up the phone, and it's my ex-girlfriend. I haven't seen her in six months. She says her husband is out with another woman. She wants to talk.

Talk to me, Lorrie, I say.

The light changes. Lorrie tells me she suspects Jack (her husband) is fucking the babysitter, the choirmaster at their church, the widow across the street, and the girl who delivers their weekend paper.

Talk to me, Lorrie, I say. Keep talking. Let it out.

The last time I saw Lorrie, we rented a cottage up north for a weekend. She left her kids (a six-year-old son, a four-year-old daughter) with a friend, and we spent seventy-two hours playing at being pioneers. Her husband had left her then, gone chasing after a stewardess to Milan, Cairo, Bombay, Singapore, but the week after we returned from the cottage, he came back to her, begging to be forgiven. Lorrie wrote me a letter and had her friend deliver it. She asked me not to call her, she wanted to make her marriage work, and I complied with her request. I never had any hard feelings for her. It was a difficult situation all around, and I didn't want to compound it.

Lorrie tells me she misses me. Her husband hasn't made love to her in a month. The kids are afraid of him. She feels like she's going crazy. She has a part-time job at the library, but with all the cutbacks, she feels sure she's going to be canned soon, so she's started to look for other work, but her computer skills aren't up to date, and she's not as thin as she used to be, and all she really wants is a couple of hundred dollars a week and to be left alone to raise her kids, but her husband is unreliable with money and she feels she's on a slide straight into the welfare trap.

Her husband asked her for a blow job the other day, and she said for a hundred dollars she would.

He asked, Are you crazy, woman?

She screamed at him that the kids needed to go to the dentist.

So take them, he said.

She asked, And who will pay?

I will, he said.

So she asked him for a blank cheque.

He asked, Are you crazy, woman?

It was vicious, brutal, and unaccountably violent.

Lorrie asks me what's new with me.

What can I say, Lorrie? I say. I've moved on.

I don't want to hear that, Gerry.

I need to be honest with you, Lorrie.

I know, she says. But I'm being honest with you, too, Gerry.

I know, Lorrie, I say. And I appreciate it. But I thought we were done. I thought we were through. Things have changed.

Gerry, she says. I don't want to hear that.

I pull up and park in front of my sister's apartment building. It has started to rain lightly. I turn the engine off and pull the keys out of the ignition. It wasn't that long ago I realized I was surrounded by women, women I wanted to meet, women I knew, women I wanted to get rid of, my sister, my mother, my boss, and I still felt a dry emptiness burning through me. I felt like everything I did was a response to a message that pumped continually through my veins. *It's not enough. Not enough.* My blood pounded in my chest, beating out this ever-present need. Once, when I was in my late teens and early twenties, it seemed all I needed to get rid of that emptiness was a night out with my friends, or a good movie, or a book, or a girlfriend, but even then the heartache always came back.

When we were kids, my sister and me, we used to pretend we were the only people left alive. The apocalypse came in many forms. Nuclear holocaust. Floods. Epidemic of a fatal disease. All life on earth was vanquished except the two of us. It seems naïve looking back on it, the two of us playing Adam and Eve, but at the time it was serious theatre. We're alone now, I would say to her. We have to look after each other. We would build forts and hunt for berries, pretend the neighbour's dog was a mutant from beyond the horizon. Often our playing ended with the two of us quarrelling, each threatening to abandon the other. Sometimes we wrestled on the grass. Sometimes we would separate, play on opposite sides of our yard, ignoring each other for hours. In my memory, we always reconciled. We need each other, don't we? she would ask.

Lorrie tells me her son's in trouble at school. He has been picking fights at recess, beating up kids smaller than him, spitting at teachers, pissing in the middle of the schoolyard. He tried to tear the clothes off a girl in kindergarten.

He needs a father, she says.

He has one, I say.

No, she says. No.

I wait for her to say something more, but she doesn't.

Hey, Lorrie, I say, finally. Can I call you back tomorrow?

After a pause, she says, Jack will be here.

I don't care if he's there or not.

I'll call you, she tells me. Then she thanks me for not hanging up on her.

Why would I do that?

I don't know, Gerry, she says. People do, though. They do, don't they?

Yes. I guess they do.

So thank you, Gerry. Thank you, she says. I'll call you tomorrow.

Sure, whatever, I say, and hang up.

When my sister was fifteen, she ran away from home. Her departure was the culmination of a series of traumas that shook our family that year. My mother admitted her alcoholism. My father denied his. They fought continually and bitterly. My uncle brought his divorce proceedings to a violent conclusion, butchering his wife and three daughters in their sleep, then shooting himself. My mother's mother suffered a heart attack, which required months of hospitalization and ultimately triple bypass surgery. My father's mother checked herself into hospital for a psychiatric assessment. The doctors found her to be suffering from high stress and anxiety. They medicated her and sent her home. Two weeks later she slipped on the ice outside her home, broke her hip and subsequently died. During those days, my sister would sneak into my room at night, and we would huddle under the covers and discuss our crazy family. Sometimes my sister made her way back to her own room. Sometimes we slept together, pressed against each other, exhausted and alone, which is how my father found us one morning when he burst in to accuse me of hiding his booze, which I sometimes did. He stopped mid-sentence, looked across at my sister, then dragged me out of bed and began kicking me up and down. I tried to cover my face, but he broke my nose. The next day, my sister disappeared.

I found out she was gone when I came home from school and my mother was standing in the middle of our front yard, her fists clenched, screaming up at the sky, tears buttering her face.

She's gone, Gerry, she said when she saw me.

I'll find her, I promised.

She's gone, she said again. Gone.

I took her by the hand and led her back in the house.

Three weeks passed before my sister called.

Don't look for me, she ordered, after confirming I was the only one home. She said she didn't want to be found. I felt I had betrayed her in some way. We talked for about five minutes, but then she said she had to go, and she hung up. All I managed to learn was that she was still in the city.

I love you, Gerry, she said, just before the line went dead.

For a month, I walked the downtown streets every chance I could, carrying a picture of my sister, handing out a Xeroxed sheet with her photo on it and my parents' phone number. I talked to dozens of street kids and winos and hookers. Whenever I'm asked for money on the street now, I think of those days and I'm hit with a mixture of sadness and anger. Poverty pulls you closer to the earth, closer to the grave. It pushes people into basements, alleys, abandoned oil tankers, the deep shadows of the city's ravines, which is where I eventually found my sister, getting out of a car at the base of Bayview. Her lipstick smeared, her minidress torn.

Hi, Gerry, she said, when she saw me. A hand reached out of the car and handed her a hundred dollars. She stuffed it in her purse and bounced towards me on her high heels. I escorted her to Eaton's. Bought her a new set of clothes. Took her to my aunt's place, which is where she stayed until she graduated from high school. Then she moved in with a defrocked priest. Two years later, she got an apartment of her own and a job answering phones for Ontario Hydro. When she met the banker (her fiancé), she was coming to the end of a series of lesbian relationships. I like men, she told me in the middle of one gin-soaked evening during that period. I want to like men. I try real hard, but sometimes I just can't.

These are my memories.

I sit in my car outside my sister's apartment building, listening to the rain. Across the street, a car pulls to a stop, parks. A figure gets out, darts across the road, rushes up the walk and through the doors. I wait. One minute, two minutes. A call comes in to my cell phone.

It's okay, my sister says, her voice full of joy. He came back. He's here.

Twelve Days
of Unemployment

Molson doesn't sell Canadian in Quebec. Did you know that?

On the first day of my unemployment, I watched sixteen hours of television. I learned that Molson doesn't sell Canadian in Quebec.

On the second day of my unemployment, I went to the Brewer's Retail for a case of Canadian. The Brewer's Retail is not called the Brewer's Retail anymore. The name on the Brewer's Retail near my place is *The Beer Store*. Well, no kidding.

On the third day of my unemployment, I ran into Dell Delorio. "Hey, Dell," I said. In grade twelve I was in love with that girl. I hadn't seen her in years. I asked her what she had been up to, but she said she couldn't stand around and talk. She had to go pick up her kid at the daycare. "Okay, Dell," I said. "Whatever. See you around." I was on my way to the video store. I wanted to get something violent. Something with a lot of explosions.

On the fourth day of my unemployment, I went to the library. I had a crush on this girl that worked at the library.

She looked like Nancy Sinatra, or Brigitte Bardot, or any of those other big–name blondes. She was probably about eighteen, or sixteen, or twenty. I couldn't tell. I wanted to talk to her, but she wasn't there, so I went home and watched TV and drank beer.

On the fifth day of my unemployment, I decided to look for a job. I bought a paper and parked myself in one of my neighbourhood's coffee shops. We're going through a coffee–shop boom, have you noticed? Everyone in the city is strung out on caffeine. It's the only drug people can afford these days. I looked through the paper and didn't find anything. Nothing matched my qualifications. The Leafs lost again. On my way home, I bought a pack of cigarettes.

On the sixth day of my unemployment, my mother phoned. I was watching a talk show about people who fall in love with teenagers who work at their local libraries, when the phone rang. "Can I call you back, Mom?" I said. "I'm in the middle of something. I'll call you right back, okay?" And I did, too. She said that she would send me some money. I took my empties to *The Beer Store* and bought some more Canadian.

On the seventh day of my unemployment, I rested.

On the eighth day of my unemployment, I made an appointment to see my dentist. I had been meaning to see my dentist for years. I don't even remember what he looks like. He only works part-time now. He's got a bunch of young dentists helping him out. My mother wanted me to become a dentist.

On the ninth day of my unemployment, I decided to volunteer at the local food bank. I didn't even know that my neighbourhood had a food bank. Then I went to the library, and there she was, pinning announcements to the "Community Events" board. FOOD BANK NEEDS VOLUNTEERS. I stood beside her and read the notice. "I never knew that there was a food bank in this neighbourhood," I said. She smiled at me. "Oh, yes," she said. "It's a neat place. I volunteer there once a month." *She smiled at me. Neat place.* I went, but she wasn't there. I helped sort the perishables from the non-perishables. I carried boxes. I handed out food.

On the tenth day of my unemployment, I started writing my film script. I had this great idea that I had been carrying around for years, but I had never put it to paper. I bought a pad of paper and began making notes. *It could take me the rest of the week*, I thought. I cracked open another beer, lit another cigarette. Worked through the night.

On the eleventh day of my unemployment, I got up at noon, then went straight back to bed.

On the twelfth day of my unemployment, I crawled into the kitchen. My head rattled like a freight train coming down a mountain. Chugga-chugga. Toot-toot. I searched the house for drugs, fruit, chicken soup. Empty cupboards, empty fridges, empties. I drank a gallon of water, wrapped myself in a blanket and thought about trudging to the food bank. I lay my head on the kitchen table. Nancy Sinatra emerged from a cardboard box which had appeared in the middle of the floor. "Do you need anything else?" she asked. "No," I heard myself say. "I'm fine, just fine."

LIONEL'S KID

Lionel says he has a kid. Jimmy, he says. That's his name. He hasn't seen him in sixteen years. He'd be eighteen, he says. If he's alive, I'm thinking, but I don't say it. There would be no point in saying it, it's obvious enough. Then he asks me for another cigarette. I'm not a smoke factory, I tell him, but I give him one anyway.

You never told me you had a kid before, Lionel, I say.

Never thought of it, he says. We all got secrets, don't we? I bet you got some secrets. But I don't answer him. Instead I ask why he thought of it now. Why did he think to tell me he had a kid now? But he doesn't want to answer that one because he's looking out the window of the coffee shop at this girl who's waiting for a bus. He just turns and stares at her. She's a blonde and she's wearing a miniskirt and a t-shirt that barely covers her breasts. I think she must have cut the thing, but Lionel says no, they make them like that now. Don't ask me why, except it's something to look at. She's something to look at, that's for damn sure. Lionel's looking at her, and I'm looking at her, too, and she doesn't see either one of us, which is probably a good thing, but I don't really give a damn and I don't think Lionel does, either.

I can see that Lionel's not going to answer my question, so I ask him if he's seen Jack around. Jack's this friend of ours, a young guy, maybe twenty, twenty-one, it's hard to tell. He got me and Lionel this job once, at the food bank, sweeping floors. They paid us, and fed us, so we're hoping it will be a regular gig. I've been back there a couple of times since, but they say they don't have any money. I got food, though, and I swept their floors for them, even though they said I didn't have to. I wanted to, though, you know. I don't like taking something for nothing, though I'm not against that, either. Some people got lots to give.

Lionel turns away from watching the girl and says he saw Jack the other day. Jack was with his wife. They were going to watch a movie. Lionel says they invited him to go with them, but he didn't want to. He said they were dressed up nice, and he didn't want to be with them. He didn't want them to feel uncomfortable, if you know what I mean. He said he forgot to ask Jack about the job at the food bank, but he said I was probably right. There was no more money, but they had food. At least for now.

I see that the bus has come and the girl's getting on it.

So much for window shopping, says Lionel.

You never stood a chance, I say, and Lionel just nods and takes a drag on his cigarette.

I bet my son's a handsome bastard. Like I was, he says. The handsomest bastard in the world, I was. And he looks at me to see if I'm going to challenge him.

I don't think that's a word, I say.

What? he says.

Handsomest. I don't think that's a word, I say. Lionel hates it when I get like this, and I can tell that he doesn't like it now.

Sure it's a word, he says. Handsome. Handsomer. Handsomest. It makes perfect sense. What's the matter with you?

I don't know, I say, but I don't feel like getting into it. So I say, it doesn't matter. Then I say something else that Lionel doesn't appreciate. You were saying that you were a pretty boy, let's talk about that. He hates that, being called a pretty boy, I can tell that right away.

I said I was handsome, he says.

The handsomest, I remind him.

Damn straight, he says. That was me.

And your son's the same, I say.

I bet you're right, he says. I bet you're damn right.

Glad we straightened that out, I say.

No problem, he says, but I can tell that he's irritated. He just doesn't want to get into it, and I don't either, really. There's nothing to be gained by it. So we just sit for a few minutes, waiting for another girl to stand on the corner and wait for the bus.

ALCHEMY

Cindy turns on the TV and falls asleep. It happens almost
that fast. She turns on the TV and changes the channel to the
all-news station. Someone is talking about the connection
between global climate change and forest fires in British
Columbia. In the corner of the screen a little box gives the
value of the Canadian dollar in US funds. The box changes
and gives the results of the day's trading on the TSE. Then
the box changes again and gives the final results on the Dow
Jones. Cindy falls asleep.

When she wakes up two and a half hours later, a
commentator is talking about the Blue Jays's extra-inning
loss to Seattle.

Cindy hits the mute button.

It has been almost four years since Cindy's last boyfriend,
James. Was James a boyfriend, or just a fuck? The first
eighteen months after they broke up Cindy thought of James
as a fuck. Then for a while she tried to forget him. Recently,
however, she has begun to think of him as a boyfriend again.

She remembers what it was like to lie on top of him, to
feel his mouth on her breast.

On the TV are images from the latest African famine. This one is in Sudan.

The next morning is Saturday.

Cindy has made a list. Three items are on the list. Do laundry. Weed garden. Buy food. Cindy sets her laundry in a basket in the hallway of her apartment. She puts her gardening gloves in her backpack and hangs the backpack on a hook by the door. She slips her bank card into the left front pocket of her shorts.

She turns the radio on and makes a pot of coffee.

Cindy would like to find a new job. She has found a half–dozen new jobs. She has gone so far as to update, print and mail her résumé, but she has yet to be invited to an interview. She first realized she didn't like her job the previous New Year's Eve, when she attended a party at a friend's house. Someone she didn't know asked her what she did for a living, and she said, "You don't want to know, you know. It's like really, really boring." Cindy sells classified ads for one of the city's major daily newspapers. She has a Bachelor's degree (Honours, 2nd class) in archaeology. She was happy to get the job. At first she told people she worked in journalism, but thirty-two months later the thrill has worn off, the conceit can no longer be upheld.

The coffee is ready. Cindy pours herself a cup. She takes her coffee out on the balcony. She wonders which is more important to her. A new boyfriend or a new job. She sees the power of the rhetoric of inclusion. She wants both. She has neither.

Cindy is twenty-six. Almost. Twenty-four was her worst birthday so far. She was suddenly closer to thirty than seventeen. Cindy sees an ambulance stuck in traffic, its lights flashing, its siren blaring. How horrible, she thinks.

The phone rings. It's Doug.

Doug is Doug Kravchek. Cindy knew Doug in high school. She met him on the street six months ago. They have become coffee and movie buddies.

"Come on, Cindy, there must be more. Yes?" her pal Dorothy asked her last week.

"No," informed Cindy.

"Not yet?" said Dorothy.

"Not never," said Cindy. "Doug's a loon."

Doug designs Web pages for an advertising company. He has a philosophy degree and a morbid obsession (Cindy thinks) with the Middle Ages. The eleventh century is of particular interest to him. Why the eleventh century? Because Ivan Illich told CBC interviewer David Cayley in 1992 that our forbears had made critical decisions in the eleventh century that have influenced the course of history ever since.

Cindy isn't sure what those decisions were. She doesn't care.

"They have to do with the relationship between humanity and technology," Doug told her once. Once was enough. She found ways to dissuade him from repeating it.

Doug played trombone in high school, Cindy the flute. Everyone had been less aware of sexism back then.

Cindy remembers Doug as a bookworm, and true to her memory that's what they spent a lot of time talking about: books. Cindy finds she can't read books by male authors. Doug insists this is ridiculous. Cindy says the only thing that's ridiculous is the way male authors try to write about women.

Cindy doesn't remember Doug ever dating, but he insists he's had a few girlfriends. She almost invited him home one night after a pint, but she thought better of it. Didn't want to lose a friend, she thought. The next morning she thought better of that, too.

Doug has come into a pair of tickets to the baseball game.

"Who's playing?" Cindy asks.

"Toronto and Seattle," Doug says.

Cindy pauses. "I don't think so. Not today."

"Give yourself a break," Doug says.

"Thanks, anyway," Cindy says.

She asks about his sister, the younger one who had her second miscarriage about ten days ago.

"She's doing okay," Doug says. "But she wouldn't tell me if things were otherwise, anyway, so I'm not a reliable source for that kind of information."

Reliable source, Cindy thinks. Jeez.

"I have to go, Doug," she says. "Good luck finding someone, though. I'll call you next week and we can arrange to do something."

She says this all the time, but she never follows through.

"Okay, bye," Doug says. He hangs up.

Doug's sister is only twenty-four. Cindy remembers her as a cheerleader in high school.

The ambulance has worked its way free. Cindy picks up her coffee on the balcony, finds it cold.

When she was a little girl, say ages six to ten, Cindy enjoyed playing the princess. *Prince O prince, where are you?* She made herself pretty, preened and waited. In university she rejected this model; she would make her own choices, refuse to be passive. She has confessed recently to Dorothy that she wants to be worshipped.

"You are a goddess," Dorothy said.

"I am," Cindy agreed.

They laughed. Where could they find men to worship them?

Cindy takes her cold coffee to the kitchen and sticks it in the microwave.

You can never tell, she thinks. Never. How things will turn out.

Last year Dorothy had been engaged. A month before the wedding her financé skipped town. Cindy imagines a headline. WORLD'S TRAGEDIES FUEL SOUL. You can never tell how things will turn out. Lead can be transformed into gold.

Poor Doug. Pour witless Doug, Cindy thinks.

Dorothy survived the loss of a husband. Cindy has never seen her better. They signed up for a course in watercolour painting. Cindy dropped out, Dorothy completed it. She has sold three paintings. *Farewell, fool husband! She triumphs from within!*

Cindy sits down in front of the TV. Turns it on. She changes the channel. Music videos. I remember this one, she thinks. 1989?

Boys and Girls, Girls and Boys

Bob called last week to say he'd been dumped by my grandmother. I said that I was sorry, it was the first I'd heard about it. I said I hoped we would still be able to see each other. I don't know why I said that. It wasn't like we were pals or anything. I didn't want him to feel too rejected, is all. Bob said he was glad I felt that way because he had enjoyed meeting me. "Just because your grandmother doesn't want to see me anymore," he said, but he didn't finish the sentence. "Yeah, sure," I said. "Maybe we can, I don't know." "Go to a movie," he said. And I said, "Why not? It could be fun." Then Bob suggested Tuesday would be a good night for him, and it so happened I was free that night, and I didn't feel like lying to this old man, who was feeling depressed and rejected already, so I said I was available and we arranged to meet at a theatre downtown. Then I called Grandma.

"Grams," I said when she finally picked up the phone. "What happened? Bob's a nice guy. What's going on?"

"I can't talk now, sweetheart," she said. "There's someone here. He's in the bathroom right now. I'll call you back, okay?"

And she hung up.

Just like that.

My grandmother's seventy-three and she's had five boyfriends since my grandfather died. That was five years ago. You do the math.

The first time I met Bob was at my grandmother's place. She's got a small apartment in a seniors' building in Scarborough, a one–bedroom with a kitchenette off the living room. I went to visit and Bob was sitting on the couch, sipping tea and enjoying a batch of my grandmother's cookies. He said he had met her when he came to visit a friend. My grandmother said it was nice to meet someone who didn't live in the building. She often complained about that, about how she didn't like her neighbours. "Why should I like them?" she would ask. "Because they're old like me?" I could see her point, but there was nothing I could do about it, so I was glad she met Bob. Also I knew that Ernie, her boyfriend at the time, had gone to Florida for the winter, so I thought she might be feeling lonely. And Bob seemed real nice, and he seemed nuts about Grandma. I remember the way he talked. Your grandmother this, your grandmother that. It was actually kind of embarrassing, but grandma ate it up.

Tuesday came before I could do anything about cancelling my appointment with Bob. I had a talk with my grandmother, though. She said Bob was nice. There was nothing wrong with Bob. But life is short, you know. And you have to enjoy yourself. Imagine my grandmother saying this to me and me trying to decide if I should tell her she had hurt Bob's feelings. As if she didn't know. As if she cared. Bob was starting to bore her, she said.

So Tuesday came and I prepared to meet Bob at the theatre. We were going to see some Hollywood comedy. I don't mind them every once in a while. I'm not nuts about them, you understand, but Hollywood's good at making stupid comedies, so you have to give them credit for that.

This one was about a waitress who gets a lottery ticket instead of a tip and the ticket turns out to be a winner.

Bob showed up right on time, wearing an overcoat and a fedora, looking very old. He said he had a hard time finding a parking spot and I was suddenly afraid for the city's drivers. I'm sure he's a fine driver, but it was supposed to rain later, and I was equally sure that Bob's reflexes were in less than top form. We made our way to the theatre and Bob said he couldn't remember the last movie he'd seen. He thought maybe it was *Singing in the Rain* with Bing Crosby. I nodded and asked what that was like, but he hit me on the arm and said that he was joking. *Singing in the Rain* came out years ago. He said that he went to movies all the time, but he usually went by himself. He used to work in the movies, he said. He'd been a film editor in Burbank before moving to Toronto with his second wife. She was from here and she wanted to be closer to her family.

"I'd been thinking of retiring," Bob said, "so we moved up here."

Then his wife died from a quickly spreading cancer. Now he was alone.

"You could go back," I said, but he said he didn't have anything to go back to. "We never had any kids, and we never made too many friends," he said. He also said my grandmother would only agree to watch videotapes with him, but he said he hated watching movies on a small screen. "I guess I'm old–fashioned," he said, but I said, "I'm with you," and then he winked at me and said, "Glad to hear it."

After the movie we were walking through the lobby of the theatre when Bob asked, "You want to go watch the girls?"

"What do you mean?" I asked.

"Don't go stupid on me," he said. "The girls, you know."

"Okay," I said.

"It's been a while," I said.

"Me, too," he said, and he winked again. He was starting to look better, I thought. If you were to ask me, I'd say he looked five years younger, at least, if that is even possible.

We got to the club soon enough and passed through a door covered with mirrors. Inside, a raunchy rock song filled the place. We passed between the tables and found a seat off to the left of the stage. A stripper was in the middle of her routine, swinging around a pole.

"What do you think?" he said, after a waitress in a halter top took our order.

"Nice," I said. "Very nice." That seemed to sum it up. What a terrific–looking woman, I thought. She was on the stage now, rolling around on a blanket. I sat up in my chair to watch her.

The waitress brought us our beers and set them on the table beside Bob's fedora. When the stripper finished her routine, Bob leaned over and tapped me on the arm.

"What did your grandmother tell you about me?" he asked.

"She said it wasn't your fault," I said.

He waved his hand in the air. "I know that," he said and gave my arm a little squeeze, real gentle, like he wanted to emphasise his point without being threatening, you know, real subtle. "But what did she tell you about *me*?"

I couldn't think of anything. "Not much," I said. "She said she was glad to meet someone from outside the building." But this didn't seem to satisfy him. I think he was after something specific, something maybe he was worried about, like a secret or something, because he turned away from me and leaned back in his chair. If it was something bad, I hadn't heard about it. My grandmother hadn't said anything, nothing that stuck out in my memory, anyway.

I excused myself to go to the bathroom. I was suddenly thinking how crazy it was for me to be sitting in a strip club with my grandmother's ex-boyfriend. It took me ages to find the bathroom, and then I just locked myself in a stall and sat there. What did he want from me, anyway? Information, friendship, someone to see movies and strippers with? He was an interesting enough guy, more interesting than some of my friends, I had to admit. He'd had a life, worked on famous movies, met some stars. Dated my grandmother. But I didn't see why the companionship role should get passed down to me. I thought I could probably come up with a hundred other places that I'd rather be than sitting off to the left of the stage with this old guy in a fedora, but then I thought hanging out with me probably wasn't his first choice, either. I sat on the john for a few more minutes, then went back out into the music.

"Not feeling well?" he asked when I got back to our table.

"No," I lied. "I probably should have stayed home tonight. Something's been going around my office. I probably should have stayed home. I don't want you to catch anything." That's it, I thought. That's how I get out of here. I started to collect my things. I pulled out my wallet and left ten dollars on the table. "Let me get it," I said. "My treat." He just sat there and watched me put on my coat. "I hope you don't get sick," I said as we shook hands. "I hope you don't catch what I've got." It seemed like he was going to stay.

The next day I told my grandmother a story about me running into Bob at the mall. I wanted to see what she would say.

"He's not well, you know," she announced. She hesitated, then continued. "He's dying."

"So that's it," I said. "That's why you don't want to see him."

She turned away from me. "Do you have time to stay for tea?"

I looked at my watch. "Yes."

"Oh good," she said. She'd done a batch of baking.

A WITNESS

A man in a black coat. The mall a streak of neon. Executing a quick sidestep, Desmond avoids two teenagers in yellow jackets. Three suits for $299. A tie store. The fountain. He sees Eaton's. Stride, stride. Six days until payday. Forces building in the Gulf. Will there be war? No, no. Hard to say. The president is frisky. Do we care? Stride, stride. Cynthia, I don't love you. I don't love you, Cynthia. I don't. There will be a scene. No, she wouldn't. Desmond is through Eaton's, the perfume, the underwear, the sweaters. On an escalator, rising.

The pub.

"How's your day?" she asks.

"Bitter. A salad of despair."

She has no clue. No clue.

"Sad," she says. "Desmond, I bought you something."

"Yes?"

A pair of earrings.

"One for you, and one for me."

"Oh, Cynthia." Now he can't. Can't. No. No.

A waitress appears. What would they like? Beer. Wine. A menu.

II

The cat licks her again. Cynthia lies on her side, her body twisted under a down comforter. She is alone in Toronto in her poorly ventilated, electric heated, sub-slum-standard student ghetto apartment. After spending her teenage years running from her family in pursuit of God, she has abandoned the church for Canada.

Cynthia pushes the cat off the bed, swings her legs free of her coverings, and picks her way between the debris scattered on the floor. She stops in the bathroom. Pushes her face to the mirror. Pulls back her cheeks. One of her men last year, her Boston men, said she had "a great mouth for pornography." She spent one night considering the consequences. She remembered a familiar lecture on Jane Austen and the value of balance: flesh and mind. She had been all spirit. Was she now to be all flesh?

After high school, Cynthia graduated to Boston College, driven by the power of a single verb—to save. Cynthia's Jesus acquired the uniform of a general. While campus feminists were *taking back the night*, Cynthia was confessing to her diary a growing fear of disease and a conviction to remain "immune." She turned to her pastor who told her only, *You are a solid disciple, Cynthia. Look forward to your life. Get married. Have some kids.* But after the comet of Christ, who was bright enough? She graduated. Then took a job at a department store and began fucking her way through the sales department.

Bob came first. A dreamer, bass player, shoe seller and peddler of fourteen variations of hashish and marijuana.

He came to see her on her second day.

"Who are you?"

"Cynthia."

"When do you get off?"

She told him and they arranged to meet. He fed her the gossip. Which managers to avoid. Which ones could be trusted. Did she want any drugs? No. They exchanged phone numbers. He called a day later and they went to a movie. She didn't know what to think of him. He was so—happy. He brought her home and got her stoned. Then the others started calling. The security guard, the janitor, the suit salesman. They treated her well. She slept with them. It seemed simple at the time.

Cynthia makes her way to her kitchen.

The cat trails her. Howls.

Cynthia turns on the radio to hear news of the sex scandal in Washington and the latest war rhetoric. She has gained a new perspective of her country since moving to Canada—and a new perspective on Canada, too. The first week after (Canadian) Thanksgiving—in October!—her mother called her. *How's the weather?* Snowing. *Well, that's what you get, Cynthia, moving up there.* It's okay, Mother, it's pretty, she had said. She had been out the night before at a faculty party, where she had met Desmond, and was feeling perky.

Cynthia pulls a bag of bagels from the fridge, removes one, slices it and throws it in the toaster. She wants Desmond to move in with her. Her neighbour, a single mother of twins, has decided that Cynthia's a lesbian, and has been trying to bed her for weeks, plying her with recipes, baseball tickets, open–ended loans of Ani DiFranco CDs.

Cynthia spoons some coffee into her Bodum, steps over the cat and throws herself into a seat by the window. It has been a dry winter. The streets are clear. The neighbourhood kids are playing ball hockey. The cat rubs against her leg.

III

Boy's night out. Desmond and Dave. Three minutes to ten, Saturday night. Desmond lines up his shot. Seven in the corner pocket. Dave takes a sip of beer. Turns to see if he can catch the score of the Leafs game on the TV in the corner of the bar.

What do young men talk about when they're alone in the city at night? The things that matter.

Desmond misses his shot. "Shit."

They have known each other since Boy Scouts, since junior high. Desmond was there when Dave's alcoholic father punched him and threw him against a wall. It was to Desmond that Dave turned when his girlfriend told him that she was pregnant; and it was Dave who Desmond asked for advice when the girl he adored turned away from him two days before the most important exam of his undergraduate career. Dave dropped out of high school a month after his seventeenth birthday. Four years later, after a series of factory and warehouse jobs, he picked up his welder's ticket. His girlfriend took his child and moved with her new lover, an ex-con, to Calgary, from where she sent him occasional poems. Letters full of stories of booze binges, petty thefts, drug deals, domestic violence. Pleas for money.

Desmond flags their waitress. Orders another beer. He has told Dave about Cynthia, but not about her request. Desmond's last girlfriend (the last woman he slept with regularly, to be more precise; what was friendly about their relationship? She once threw a salt shaker at him; he used up the thesaurus looking for words to abuse her with) had moved to South America two years ago to work with a community development agency on an agriculture project for peasants. They had spent six high-anxiety, high-pleasure weeks living together in a house–sit in Rosedale, enjoying their hosts' extensive World Music CD collection and incubating a mutual hatred that exploded after a night of fierce lovemaking when

Desmond prepared omelettes and attempted to lightheartedly explain away the lack of mushrooms. He'd forgotten to buy them. *Imbecile.* The next day his girlfriend moved out and spent a fortnight calling to complain about his body odour. His reading habits. The size of his dick.

Desmond hasn't seen Dave in a month. Before Cynthia began to talk about co-habiting.

"Your shot." Dave hands Desmond the cue.

Desmond turns and gets a good look at the woman beside the bar. She looks like someone he knows, knew. Who? She looks like an actress, like someone he saw recently on David Letterman. He can't remember. He plays his shot. Misses.

On TV the Leafs are being brought down by their weak defence.

Dave takes the cue from Desmond and sinks his three remaining balls. They surrender the table and retreat.

"Listen," Dave says. "I met this guy, right? He drives a forklift. I met him at the First Aid at work. I was there for a cut, and he was there for something, I don't know what, and we got to talking, and he told me about this place he goes. He's been there a couple of times. It's a spa like, that sort of place. Okay?"

"Right," Desmond says. "You went?"

"I went."

"Okay."

"Very strange, my friend."

Desmond takes a sip of beer. "What happened?"

"I'm not saying what happened."

"What did you see?"

"Everything."

"Like?"

"Everything, man. There was a pool. People were in the pool, people were beside the pool. People were doing it. You name it. The place had a dozen little rooms. You want privacy, they got privacy. You want people to watch, people will watch."

Desmond nods. "You like to watch?"

"No." Dave laughs. "I can't believe you, man." He punches Desmond on the shoulder.

"What?"

"I tell you my story, and you say *that*."

"What? It's a legitimate question."

"Sure."

"Right."

Dave starts over: "What I was trying to tell you was, I went to this place, and I couldn't believe that I was there. I couldn't believe that such a place existed."

"Oh, I see."

"Got it?"

"Yes, I think so." Did he? No, but he knew that was all he was going to get.

The woman at the bar is looking their way. Desmond smiles, but she doesn't respond.

When he entered university, Desmond thought the world owed him something. When he was twenty-one, he became depressed for a year. He drank. Wore black. Took up smoking. Filled two notebooks with obsessive, self-pitying poetry. It was the poetry, he told Cynthia, that saved him. "It was bad!" His soul has a lyrical quality that he has found hard to satisfy; the poetry showed him its outline, drove him in on himself, into his shadows. He wanted to believe that there was something that would give him those feelings of transcendence that he used to get as a teenager. Looking out over a northern lake, under the stars, listening for a loon, feeling intimately connected to the inner workings of the universe. Above life, floating. When had he last felt like that? He wanted to believe in love as a saving power. But he didn't.

He graduated from university and spent two years stacking shelves in a big–box bookstore. The job provided his beer money. The job paid off his student debt. Then he signed up for a series of Information Technology courses at a community college and landed a job checking computer codes for the Y2K bug, the Millennium Virus.

Desmond sees the woman from across the bar walking towards him.

"Hi." She's carrying a pack of cigarettes.

"Hi."

"My friend," the woman says. She turns and points to a woman who had been standing beside her, a brunette with big hair wearing a leather miniskirt and an Armani suit jacket. "My friend wants to know if you're seeing anyone."

Desmond says, "No."

"What's your name?"

He tells her.

"Her name is Katherine. Here's her phone number." She opens the cigarette pack and pulls out a slip of paper.

"Thanks."

The woman smiles and walks back across the bar.

IV

"I can't live with her."

They have migrated to Desmond's place, opened a bottle of whiskey.

"Desmond. Come on, man." Dave can't see the big deal.

"Move in with her or don't, but don't drag me into this."

Desmond pours them two more shots. He feels too old for this kind of conversation. Boy meets girl. Boy loses girl. He hasn't lost Cynthia yet, but he feels her slipping away. He doesn't want to lose her. What is this? *A feeling of affection.* Dave has already asked about their bedroom performance (not that that's all that matters, but it's a big part; and who will deny that it isn't significant?). *Are you satisfied?* Desmond assured him that that was not the problem. *So?* So moving in with her didn't *feel* right. *Oh, really*. Yes. But he did feel something; there was sentiment there, evidently. He couldn't just walk away.

When they had met at the pub, Desmond had every intention of breaking it off, but Cynthia had bought them earrings, and then there was her face. He enjoyed looking at it, the bowls of her cheeks, the curve of her nose, the shards of green in her eyes.

He makes his way to the kitchen to fill a bowl with ice cubes.

"It's a boundary issue," he tells Dave when he gets back, setting the bowl on the table beside the cable converter. Dave reaches for an ice cube and drops it in his glass.

"I need my space," Desmond says.

"Sure."

"I have to be able to respect myself."

"Right."

"I'm not ready for this."

"Okay."

The first thing he remembers them talking about is J.D. Salinger's *Franny and Zooey*. At the faculty party where they met he asked Cynthia about her favourite author. Who was he or she? She answered: J.D. Salinger. What surprised Desmond was that she didn't name *Catcher in the Rye* as her favourite Salinger book; instead she gave the award to *Franny and Zooey*. "Why?" Her answer was instantly intimate: "I wanted what Franny wanted. When I read it, I felt *she is me*. I knew exactly how she felt when she was sitting in the restaurant talking to her boyfriend who *just didn't get it*, and how she wanted to disappear into spiritual bliss, how she wanted to escape the everyday humdrum, the decline of civilization as we know it."

"From Plato to Disney," Desmond had said, which caused her to laugh.

"Yes. I suppose. You're agreeing with me, right? I'm very insecure when I first meet people. I always figure that they're making fun of me."

"Not at all," Desmond assured her.

"So you agree with me."

"Absolutely." Their relationship had begun.

Desmond sips his whiskey and turns on the television. If it's true that in the beginning of every relationship are the seeds of its destruction, then he figures that a glance in the rear–view mirror might be all the wisdom that he requires. He tosses the converter at Dave, who doesn't move as it bounces off his chest.

Cynthia's occasional mysticism was a concern. Like Franny, she sometimes seemed to be seeking an other-worldly experience. But she was no New Age freak. Crystals and the Tarot had no place with her, though she enjoyed burning incense and covered the walls of her apartment with silkscreens. He knew about her teenage fling with Jesus, a common obsession. There was obviously a streak of Puritanism in her, common enough, he thought, among Americans, especially those from New England. He wasn't frightened by Cynthia's religious bug the way many people he knew would have been; true religious experience was a celebration of the fullness of life, he knew that, but he also knew many people who saw in religion only a hell-and-brimstone morality. What concerned him about Cynthia was that she sometimes appeared to pull herself out of life altogether. They talked about that, about spirituality as escape. Desmond told her how he used to dream about flying over northern Ontario. Not in an airplane, and not in his body he didn't think: just his spirit or his soul gliding over lakes and forest, rocks and swamps. Cynthia told him how she used to believe that the truth would set her free, but now she thinks freedom can only come in spurts. Bondage was an important part of the real world. Bondage to your friends, your family, your community. Your God.

"Check this out."

Dave has changed the channel. On the screen is a man massaging a woman's breast. She is lying on a couch. He is kneeling. She is wearing a white silk shirt which has been unbuttoned and fallen open. They are speaking Italian. Once when he was at university, he came home from the bar on a Friday night to his dorm and found a group of guys watching a blue movie on TV. No one in the room understood the language. He stood in the doorway until the action on the screen built up to the sex scene, after which the lounge emptied and he changed the channel to watch music videos.

Dave asks, "Are you going to call her?"

"Who?"

"That woman from the bar," Dave says.

"No."

"So why did you take the number then?"

"I don't know. I was hoping that it was for the other woman."

"Why would you take *her* number?"

"Why not?"

"Because you're torn apart by guilt about not moving in with this Cynthia chick."

The woman on the screen sits up. She unbuttons the man's pants. The scene shifts to a bedroom. A bed. The couple enter through a doorway. The screen turns blank, followed by a commercial. Dave changes the channel. Hockey highlights.

"I don't want to move in with her," Desmond says.

"I think you do."

"I don't."

"I think you do."

"I don't."

"I think you do, but you think you can't."

"Exactly right."

The whiskey has settled into his spine. Exactly right. He wants to, but he doesn't think that he can. Why not? Through the whiskey he can't see a reason, and he knows that he'll do it. How will it end? With Cynthia falling for a

tree–hugger and moving to British Columbia. With
Desmond getting pushed in front of a subway train. With
Desmond developing a sudden and severe allergy to cats.

None of the above.

V

Cynthia turns off the radio and stares out her kitchen
window. The United Nations has brokered a deal to keep
the US war machine out of Iraq.

Desmond has moved in.

The phone rings.

It's Penny, one of Cynthia's classmates. They had spent
the previous afternoon together after Cynthia found her
bawling in the library.

Penny has boy trouble.

"I just wanted to thank you."

"Don't," Cynthia says. "It's okay. Really."

"I need to. You were great to me."

"Okay."

Penny pauses. Silence. "Thank you."

Cynthia waits.

"You're welcome," she says.

Penny: "I was wondering—"

"Yes?"

"—if I could talk to you again sometime—soon."

She's a dysfunctional dip. That was Desmond's opinion
upon hearing Cynthia recount her three and a half hours
with Penny. A dysfunctional dip, maybe, but a beautiful one,
Cynthia told him. Bring her home, Desmond joked. Penny
wore her blonde hair in curls, her jeans torn and faded; her
insecurities more prominent than the jewellery hanging
between her often half–exposed breasts. She sang in a band
outside of school. Cynthia heard about how she had carried

on a concurrent affair with the drummer and the bass player until the three of them decided to set aside their passions except for the music. Now she was having a fling with a PhD student in one of her classes, but she had decided the day before yesterday that she was in love with her postmodernism professor, who was a woman and brilliant, "so brilliant"; meanwhile, an old boyfriend from Montréal had shown up a month ago, and she had slept with him, and he wanted her back, and he kept phoning her, and she had slept with him again, "but only for one last time. I made that clear," but he had declined to hear her, and still he kept phoning.

"My goodness," Cynthia had said.

"I'm a busy girl."

Three and a half hours they spent together. Penny talked about her men, the professor she wanted to bed, the paper that she couldn't get off the ground.

"I'm a witness to love," Penny said. "You got to give it out, if you want to get it back—and you got to get it back!"

Cynthia told her about a scene that she had observed recently on the subway. She was sitting on the end of a row of seats beside a couple who were speaking a foreign language. Russian, probably.

"They were dressed in hand-me-down clothes, probably picked up from a second–hand store or handed out from a refugee centre. A church basement somewhere. That's what struck me first, but then I heard them speaking and I was transported to Moscow. For a flash, just an instant, I imagined that the subway train was rumbling through Moscow. You see documentaries or news stories about Russia from before the fall of communism or after, and the narrative is the same: people struggling with deprivation. The couple beside me were still struggling, even though they had found a way to Toronto. But I noticed one thing: they were holding hands. And as I listened to them, I felt that they were singing a love song. The inflections of their voices, the way they moved towards each other, the way they looked at each other. When I got off the train, the image of them lingered in my mind. I thought that I had never seen a more passionate couple."

Giving it out and getting it back. Cynthia carried the phrase home with her after she left Penny waiting for a meeting with her PhD fuck buddy.

Cynthia pulls three eggs out of the refrigerator and begins to make an omelette.

"Okay," she had said to Penny. "I'll meet you again, but not today." Today is her day with Desmond.

Three weeks ago he moved in. How has it been? Nice. Warm. Comfortable. What had surprised her was how often they talked. They talked all the time, and not only about them, the relationship. When they had been seeing each other (but not living together), he hadn't talked much. Now she had discovered in him caverns of conversation. When she asked him about it, he said, "You ask good questions."

Cynthia hears Desmond in the bathroom. She chops two mushrooms and throws them in a frying pan.

DORIAN

Dorian took two weeks to ask me. He works in the booth beside mine. The first time we talked, I thought he was pretty dull. He got better, though. Persistence pays off. His and mine both. We started eating our lunches together, and then he asked me. So we're going out.

Dorian wears nice sweaters. That's the first thing I noticed about him. He's got a great collection of sweaters, and he's always got his nose in a book. What are you reading, Dorian? I think those are the first words that I ever said to him. The supervisor had introduced him to the other telemarketers the day before. It's a book about the future of Canadian culture, Dorian said. He was pretty excited about it. It's nice to talk to a guy who's interested in ideas. For a change, you know. I finished school two years ago. Bachelor of Arts, Psychology. I thought I was glad to get off the academic treadmill, but when I talk to Dorian, I kind of miss the Ivory Tower. I miss being stimulated that way. I don't have too many intellectual spark plugs in my life. Dorian is still working on his degree part-time. History with a Minor in English Literature. So it's easier for him.

I told my mother about Dorian, and she said he reminds her of my father.

"Don't let him bring a book to bed," she said.

"Ma," I said. "Relax. It's just a date."

Six months ago I brought a guy home to meet my mother, and she wasn't impressed. She thought he was an idiot, is what I'm saying. So I thought the fact that I was going on a date with an intellectual would make her happy.

"Life's not so simple," she said to me. "You can't just go from one extreme to the other. You need to choose your apples carefully. Not too tender. Not too fresh."

Yes, apples. My mother compared men to apples.

"I have a degree in psychology, Mother," I said. "I know something about people."

"You know nothing," she said, and not for the first time. "They teach you nothing. You learned so much, but still you make these terrible mistakes."

II

Dorian has blue eyes. Very pretty blue eyes you have, Dorian, I said. We were near the end of our meal. Dorian took me to a tiny Italian place. Candles on the tables, good wine, the appropriate music. I like your eyes, Dorian, I said. We had tickets for the theatre. We had spent most of our dinner talking about The Fate of the Left in Canadian Politics. Dorian was concerned; I was indifferent. I paid a lot of attention to his eyes, which swam with waves of passion. For me or The Left, though, I wasn't sure.

When I told him that I liked his eyes, he blushed. Good Lord, I could have jumped him right there. I slid my hand over to his, and we locked fingers.

Last year I was in a relationship with a guy who beat me. Twice he beat me. We fought. I lost. I thought I loved him. I did love him. That's why I stayed after the first time. I wanted to help him. I wanted to be there. Where? I saw his weakness, and I wanted to fix it. But when he blamed me for the fights, when he wouldn't promise me that he would change, when he didn't even try, I left. It was hard, but I did it. Gone, buddy. I'm history. You have to take responsibility for your own shit. I'm very big on that. Sometimes I think about what happened, and it seems like a previous incarnation.

Dorian says it's terrible what happened, but what I want him to see is that we cared for each other, me and Mark. We fought, but we stood up for each other. Until near the end. With Dorian, though, things are different. He's the sweetest guy I've ever known, but I have a hard time getting a hold of him. He floats. He hides. He's very self-reliant. It's like a game, and sometimes I enjoy it—looking for Dorian—and sometimes I wish that he were more like Mark.

III

You should see my breasts. They hang off my chest like a pair of dried prunes. They sag, they stand up, they point north and south, they get tender, feel limp, rage with desire, ache with a dull rumble which is tied to the orbit of one of the planets we haven't discovered yet. My breasts are pathetic, is what I'm saying.

Dorian's shy about his body, so I made him join my fitness club. Spend a couple hours a week at the gym, I told him, and you'll feel like a million bucks. He's toning up a bit, too; his chest feels a little less like gelatin, which I like, and I told him so. You look fabulous, Dorian, I said, and let me tell you, he's getting sexier all the time.

The first time that I got him into bed, brother. It was nearly a disaster. After the theatre I led Dorian to a pub for a late-evening paralyser, then asked him to walk me home.

You will come up, won't you? I asked (I want you, Dorian, I do, I do). I stood on the bottom step and brushed his hair behind his ears. I don't like going into an empty house, I said. Of course, he said. He came up. I took his coat, lit a half-dozen candles, turned the lights down low. You do like me, don't you, Dorian? I asked. He leaned over to kiss me and caught me on the side of the nose. Sorry, he said. Hallelujah! A romantic moment. No, no, Dorian, I said. It's okay, it's okay. But he backed away, then he started apologizing again, and I told him to sit down, and he did, and I stood in front of him, my knees between his knees, and I pulled off my sweater and unbuttoned my blouse. Then I leaned forward and kissed him, and kissed him, and kissed him.

IV

My mother wanted to meet Dorian. He's doing things to you, she said. You bet, I almost blurted. But it was no joke. I told Dorian to be prepared.

He brought roses. Oh sweetheart! My mother sat him down in the living room: underneath the portrait of her parents, beside the table which held her icon of the Holy Virgin, on top of the quilt that she alone had sewn and which she had spread across the chesterfield only the day before. Roses in her arms, cradled more lovingly than any baby, my mother perched herself on the edge of the wooden rocking chair that has graced our parlour since I was making my way steadily through a forest of disposable diapers. I was sent to find a vase.

"That's so considerate," Momma said, gushing.

Dorian handed her the flowers.

"Don't forget to offer your guest a drink," Momma threw after me, as I trundled off to procure a container.

Dorian was explaining millennial angst to my mother when I returned.

"He is a smart man, this boy," Momma said, her lips puckered, her head nodding fiercely.

I took the roses from her, unwrapped them, and placed them one by one in the vase I had found covered in a heavy layer of dust underneath the kitchen sink.

"Yes, Momma," I said. "What has he been telling you?"

"Everyone thinks that the world is ending, we feel like the world is ending," she said. "The end of the century, the dying of the century, we feel like we are dying, we feel like the world is falling apart, but this happens always at the end of centuries. After the year 2000, we will feel like we are being reborn."

"That's interesting, Momma," I said. She smiled at me and asked me why I hadn't brought in the chocolates.

"I forgot," I said.

"So go get them," she said.

Dorian was quizzing my mother about the quilt when I entered carrying the chocolates.

"The colours are so well balanced," he said.

"I am very careful," said Momma.

"No kidding," I said. I had just raised a chocolate to my mouth. Momma reached out and struck me on the back of my head.

"Ignorant girl," she said.

She pulled her hand back, crossed it with her other and piled them in her lap.

"You cannot trust this one," she said to Dorian, reigning in her hurt. "She has a fast lip and a simple mind. You should not put your faith in her. She cannot hold it."

V

Dorian kisses me again.

"Finish your story," I say. He has been telling me about a friend, a young man unlucky in love. His friend falls for women who exude (in Dorian's words) "a potent and dangerous mix of victim ideology and wilful self-destruction." Sounds painful, I said. I could hardly control myself. I thought it was one of the funniest things that I had ever heard him say.

"Downright lethal," I say, which is when he kisses me.

Dorian's friend falls for women who blame him for their faults. He wants their pain, says Dorian. He wants to fix them. O warrior. O great knight! Rescue dear maidens from their neuroses.

O master of chivalry!

"Then what happened, Dorian?" I say. He tells good stories, so I know that he is going somewhere with this one. "What happened next?"

Watching Parking Metres (The Quality Lit Game)

It was another normal city on another normal day. The author sat in the Green Room, psyching himself up for another television interview. The makeup woman had prepared his face with indifference. She sees so many famous people, he thought. Not that he was famous. His first novel had appeared six months earlier and it was selling moderately well. The makeup woman probably had no idea who he was, he thought. Nor did she care.

The show he was about to appear on was a daytime talk show. A new one, one he hadn't heard of until the week before when his publisher had called him and said the show's producers were looking for a writer to appear on a panel. "We think this is a great opportunity," his publisher had said, and the author tended to agree. He had been on TV before, but never with so large a potential audience.

A large woman in overalls stuck her head in the door.

"Ten more minutes."

"Thank you," said the author.

He picked a copy of his novel off the coffee table and gripped it tightly. The book was about a gang of teenage boys who terrorized an urban neighbourhood until an ecological disaster threatened their region and a rock–star goddess recruited them to combat the environmental threat. He had started the story as his undergraduate thesis project at a large eastern university, where a supportive professor had encouraged him to send it to a friend who was a literary agent. A publishing deal quickly materialized and eighteen months later the author was making the circuit, peddling his catalogue of one.

He had his finger up his nose when they called again to tell him they were one minute from going on the air.

The large woman in overalls ushered him to his seat.

"We're looking for some sparks today," she said.

The author nodded. He had been warned by his publisher to remain cool.

"Television is a cool medium," his publisher had advised him. "Remember McLuhan: television, cool; radio, hot."

The woman in overalls clipped a microphone to the author's jacket.

"Go gettem, cowboy," she said, patting him on the shoulder.

The author observed the audience, who appeared to be placidly awaiting instruction. I thought I was going to be part of a panel, he thought. There were three other chairs on the platform, but they were all unoccupied.

A man with a clipboard, whom the author assumed to be one of the show's producers, stood in front of the audience and began counting down with his fingers. Five, four, three, two. When he flashed his final finger, the show's host appeared from backstage to waves of applause from the audience. The show's theme music blared and the author turned to see the woman in overalls ushering a pair of women behind the cameras and pointing to the two empty seats beside him. The first woman was short, heavyset, and wearing a black spandex miniskirt; the second (tall and thin) wore an expensive pinstripe suit (an Armani?) and big hair.

The author stuck his finger up his nose.

"Welcome," said the host, his smile the strength of a thousand suns.

The audience roared.

"Today," said the host. "Today we are lucky to have on our show Gene McMichaels, an expert in gang violence and environmental disasters."

An "applause" sign flashed and the audience roared again.

An expert, thought the author. Me? Can't hurt the book sales, huh. He had already decided to behave in a professorial manner, to project a demeanour appropriate to a "serious young novelist."

The host announced the first commercial break, then approached the author and introduced the two strange women, who had followed the host on to the stage.

"Gene," the host said, his eyes like pale moons. "It's good to finally meet you. I've heard so much about you. You know Gretta and Mimi, of course."

"I'm afraid not," said the author. "Regretfully," he added. Should he?

"Gretta Rogers and Mimi Garbot," said the host.

"Oh, yes," Gene said. It seemed best.

He shook hands with the women, who took up positions in the seats beside him. They smiled at each other silently until the commercial break ended, the audience applauded and the host began to introduce them to the audience.

As the audience's applause dwindled, Mimi, the stocky woman in the miniskirt, leaned across the author and whispered to Gretta: "Bitch."

A camera swung around in front of them, and the host said, "Gretta and Mimi are with us again." The author noted hoots and whistles from the audience as the host held up a copy of the author's book and asked Gretta what she thought of it.

"Pablum," Gretta said.

Mimi snarled.

"Be fair, Gretta," the host said, his skin glowing like a Cuban beach. "Gene here has written a serious book about a serious issue, a serious study with serious consequences."

"The book is manure," Gretta said.

"It's mud unfit for pigs," she added when the host, his microphone tucked under his chin, paused to give her time to expand on her initial assessment.

The host nodded. "Okay, Gretta. Thank you," he said.

He turned to Mimi.

"Mimi," he said, his hair more solid than the Lincoln Monument. "We count on you for balancing opinion. What did you think of the book?"

"Actually, Stanley," Mimi said. She said it in a drawl that the author couldn't place until a violent thought sprang into his mind. Mr. Howell! From *Gilligan's Island!*

"I didn't like it, either," Mimi continued.

"Can you tell us why?" the host said.

"The book," said Mimi, "is obviously a projection of Mr. McMichaels's deep fantasies. Frankly, I found it deranged and pornographic. Mr. McMichaels uses the rubric of environmental salvation to reinforce the domination of the active male over the passive female, of Chaos over Nature."

"Mimi, Mimi," the audience chanted.

Mimi continued: "The gang violence is nothing more than a metaphoric representation of Mr. McMichaels's unrestrained id, his subconscious desire to lash out at the world, which can only be controlled by a fantasy figure, a literal Venus who returns to the modern world from ancient mythology in the form of a voluptuous rock goddess, though she turns out to be a powerless, paper-thin construction who cannot save the world herself but must yoke herself to the forces of male violence already at large in the land."

The host walked around behind the author and put his hands on his shoulders.

"Gene," said the host, his voice warmer than a Mediterranean summer night. "It looks like you're in trouble with the ladies."

"Mimi, Mimi," the audience chanted.

"Well, you know," said the author. He tried to remember an insight Terry Southern had made years ago about "the quality lit game," but instead found himself mumbling something about Bob Dylan and watching parking metres.

"Save it, Gene. Save it," said the host. "We'll get back to you right after—" the host looked up and pointed at the camera "—this commercial break."

The host smiled, the audience roared, Gretta lean across the author and whispered to Mimi: "Slut."

The author put his finger up his nose.

The woman in overalls returned to the stage, carrying a tray with three glasses of water on it. The author picked up a glass and promptly dropped it on the floor. When the show was ready to begin again, he realized that he had completely forgotten his previous line of defence. He sat with his head in his hands, trying to remember the lexicon from a course he had taken in feminism and postmodernism. Hadn't it been male/order and female/chaos? Hadn't it been the Freudian phallus, the one, the singular, the sure, that feminism had deconstructed ("de-cunt-structed," in the words of his professor) in favour of the subjective, mysterious, complex . . . cunt? He felt certain that his memory was correct; equally certain that it didn't matter; his credibility with the studio audience was shot to Hades.

The author thought he heard a bell. The show began again.

"Before you respond, Gene, to what Gretta and Mimi had to say earlier," the host said, his tongue sliding across his teeth like Chinese silk, "tell us about your book. Tell us," the host paused, "about what your book means to our society and the lives of the people sitting here today."

"I'm glad you asked me that," the author said. He was

stunned. His publisher had led him to believe that writers were never asked such sensible questions.

He tried a joke.

"The truth is," he said, "I wrote it for the money."

"It shows," Gretta interjected.

"Thank you, Gene," the host said.

"I'm not finished," said the author.

"The big pencil is going for the big spurt," said Mimi. The audience cheered.

"That's not fair," said the author.

"No?" said Mimi.

"It's not his balls, it's his puny brain," said Gretta.

The author bit his tongue. "Where I come from," he said, "they're called Jacobian chestnuts." He no longer knew what he was saying.

"Time for questions from the audience," the host said, his glee overflowing like Mount St. Helen's in full blow.

The host wandered into the audience.

"Who would like to speak?" he asked.

A short, anorexic woman in a peach sweat top and orange shorts stood up and grabbed the micophone.

"Thank you, Stanley," she said. "I'd just like to say . . . I'd like to say to that man, that author . . . what a disgusting person he is."

"And why is that, Madam?"

"Huh?" The woman lifted her cheekbone up past her ear, closed one eye and stared contemptuously at the host with the other.

"Why is Gene disgusting, Madam?"

"He's a whore, that's why," the woman said. "Making money off the blood of our inner cities. It's flat disgusting. He ought to be ashamed. People live in those rats' nests. Real people, Stanley. Real people with real lives, and along comes Mr. I-Think-I'll-Write-A-Book and he's off printing money with the blood of them gangs' victims."

"Thank you, Madam," said the host.

The author stared impassively into the lens of the camera nearest him. He felt sure the producers were watching him for a reaction.

"Shame, shame," chanted the audience.

A college–age student in a Spice Girls t-shirt stood up and took the microphone.

"Like I agree with Gretta, okay?" she said.

The host stood beside her, nodding.

The girl continued: "I haven't read it or anything, but I think the book we're talking about or whatever is like dirt that not even pigs would eat, okay? Not even pigs. Can you imagine how bad that is, okay? Not even pigs will eat it, and pigs will eat anything, okay? So that's very totally like real bad. I don't even know why you had him on your show, you know. It's so obvious that he's obviously got nothing to say."

The author smiled in the way his mother often told him was charming.

The host made his way down one aisle, across the front of the stage, and up another aisle where a middle-aged woman in a blue polka–dot dress was standing with her arm in the air. The host handed her the microphone.

"Thank you, Stanley," she said, then she turned to look at the author.

She looks like a librarian, the author thought. Too bright for her station in life. Too self-sufficient to bother about a husband. Too organized to generate an original thought.

"Gene," the woman said. "I've listened carefully to the various comments that have been made here today, and on the whole I find them fair and reasonable. I am concerned, however, that you haven't said enough. In particular, I'm interested in your background. Your family system, in other words. Your birth sequence: were you born first, second, third? Were there any major family crises during your childhood? Did your father change jobs, for example? Was he laid off, bored, having an affair perhaps? I don't feel it's fair to judge your book until we get to know a little about you. Who are you, Gene? Could you tell us that?"

"How about it, Gene?" said the host, who had retrieved the microphone.

The librarian had a wide-mouth grin on her face. She stood staring at the author, then she sat down.

"I'm sorry, I can't," said the author. "I try to keep my private life and my professional life separate."

"I bet he smokes drugs," said Gretta.

"I bet he likes guns," said Mimi.

The librarian was still smiling.

"Okay," said the host. "That's it, we're almost out of time."

The audience broke into applause.

"Next week," said the host, his mind drifting like the tides on the Bay of Fundy, "next week Gretta and Mimi will tell us what to think about those unfathomable stock markets and the sexy international intrigue of global derivatives traders."

"Mimi, Mimi," the audience chanted.

The author smiled bravely into the nearest camera until he was sure the show was over, then he stood, unpinned the microphone from his jacket and stuck his finger up his nose.

Gretta slapped him on the back.

"You did great, Gene," she said.

"Yes, truly," Mimi said. She grabbed his hand and shook it. "Would you like to join us for a drink?"

The author could hardly believe it.

"The three of us?" he said.

"Sure, Gene," said Gretta.

"It was only a show, man," said Mimi. "Don't take it personal."

She reached behind him and grabbed his ass.

WORKING IT OUT

Three hours out of the city, Joan and Dave arrive at the cottage outside of Wasaga Beach that they have on loan from friends of a friend, only to find themselves locked out.

"The keys," says Dave, looking back at Joan, who is starting to unpack the car. "Do you have the keys?"

"I thought you had them." She lifts another suitcase out of the trunk.

"I don't have them," Dave says.

"So you don't have them," says Joan. "Check under the mat."

"There is no mat," says Dave.

"Then check in the mailbox."

But there's no mailbox, either, only a flap in the door, which Dave lifts. He gets down on one knee and peers inside. Two chairs sit on opposite sides of a weathered card table. A pair of beaten leather sandals rests against the wall.

"I'm going to look around the other side," says Dave. "Maybe there's an extra key in the boathouse."

He walks along the right side of the cottage and down a stone path to the water. Out on the lake a loon makes a splash and disappears under the surface. Dave waits a minute to see where it will reappear. The bird pops up a hundred yards further along the shore. A fibreglass canoe lies to the right of the path, chained to a tree. He looks underneath the boat to see if it's hiding a tackle box or something, anything that might hold a key, but there is nothing there.

"Well?" says Joan when Dave returns. She's sitting on the car hood smoking a cigarette.

"Nothing," says Dave.

He reaches into the breast pocket of Joan's shirt and takes out the pack of cigarettes.

"No boathouse, no keys," he reports.

"Great," says Joan. "What a great start to the weekend."

"Please don't be like that." Dave takes a cigarette out of the package and looks at Joan. It's their second anniversary, and he's not sure that he knows her. "It's going to work out. This is going to be the weekend of things working out."

"Yes, I know," says Joan. "You keep saying that, but look where we are now."

She waves her hand out in front of her and looks up at the trees that surround them.

Dave places the cigarette gently between his lips and lights it. He wants to quit smoking, and he wants Joan to quit with him, but Joan says she will only quit if she gets pregnant. Dave pulls the smoke deeply into his lungs and lets it out slowly. It's killing him, and he knows it, but for the moment it feels good.

"Maybe there's a window I can force open," he says, but he doesn't move.

Joan takes another drag on her cigarette. Her hair blows in front of her face. She's growing it again, trying to make it like it was when they first met. Dave is glad about this, but he didn't ask her to do it. That's why he's glad, he guesses. He had even told her that he liked her face, and when her hair was short he could see more of it. That's what he told her, but she said she was going to grow her hair anyway because she knew he liked it long, no matter what he said now.

"Okay, Mr. Break-and-Enter," Joan says. "Check it out."

Dave finishes his cigarette and then disappears behind the cottage. A minute later he opens the front door from the inside.

"My husband the felon," Joan says, and laughs. Dave laughs, too, and for the first time he feels that coming to the cottage was a good idea. Maybe things would work out.

He leans against the doorframe and chuckles. Joan slides off the car, walks toward him and wraps her arms around his waist, tilting her face up towards his until he bends down and kisses her.

"You're the best," she says. "We're going to have fun, aren't we? This is going to be a blast."

"Absolutely," says Dave.

He kisses her again and slips his hand under her t-shirt. She steps back from him, and he runs his fingers across her belly, rolls his thumb around her navel, then spreads his hand across her left breast and lightly pinches her nipple. Joan takes hold of his shoulders, and they kiss again. Then she unbuttons his jeans and pushes him through the door and into the cottage.

"First things first," she says. "Where's the bed?"

They both laugh and follow each other through an open door on the left side of the room. Clothes fall to the floor, and they throw themselves onto a yellowed foam mattress spread out under the window.

"I'm ready," she says.

"Today?"

"Today's the day," she says.

He feels certain that today *will* be the day, the day it happens, the day the future stops seeming so far away. He feels this suddenly and with certainty, though not for the first time. Something always gets in the way, holds them up, diverts them, drives them apart; or it pulls them back into the past, or reminds them where they are in the present, and what they're struggling against. Then there's the weight he feels in his mind and how it pounds against the inside of his head and how hard it is to come home from work at the end of the day.

They lie beside each other when it's over, naked, listening to the birds.

"I felt something," she says.

"Did you?"

"Yes."

"Me, too," he says, wanting to believe it, but mostly he feels hungry. And then he remembers that they forgot to stop for groceries on the way.

THIRTEEN SHADES
OF BLACK AND WHITE

The plane banks to the left. Sean holds the paperback he bought at the airport in Vancouver between his thumb and index finger, marking his spot. He peers over the shoulder of the lawyer beside him. A million lights cover the ground, sparkling like a perpetual firecracker. He strains to see the lake and the tower that pins the city to the water, a shower of light clinging to the darkness.

The lawyer says, "Impressive, isn't it?"

He nods.

"I'm amazed every time," she says. She can't be much older than he is, he thinks. He's nineteen. Maybe she's thirty. Must be at least that. Looks young for her age. Looks about twenty-five. She has already told Sean that she's a litigator, working for one of the country's major banks. Her briefcase is open on her knees. She's wearing a skirt over black stockings and a sharp green vest. She folds the file she's been reading, slides it under a stack of papers and clicks the case closed.

It is mid-November, and he has told her he is on his way home for Christmas.

"So soon?"

He shrugged. His professors knew what was happening, and his roommate, but that was all.

The plane prepares for its final approach. The seat–belt lights flash on, and the stewards tell everyone to get ready and make their way to their positions.

He turns to glance out the window. The lawyer is looking at him.

"Is it a girl?"

"Excuse me?"

"Sorry. You don't have to tell me," she says. "I just thought I'd ask. It's good to talk. You look strained."

She waits. He looks out the window and sees the outlines of buildings. Cars rush along the city's arteries.

The stories he could tell.

"I'm okay," he says.

The plane hovers 100 metres off the runway for what seems like half an hour, then they touch down with a thud. The brakes squeal. Sean feels gravity grip him as air tears around the plane, fracturing his sense of drifting with a tremendous roaring sound, returning him solidly to the earth.

"I'm okay," he says, attempting a smile.

The lawyer squeezes his arm.

2

His father is asleep.

Damn you, he wants to say.

His father lies still, tubes protruding from his veins, a monitor above his bed beeping with every beat of his heart.

Damn you. I'm not through with you.

From behind the curtain that separates his father's bed from the one occupied by the other patient in the room, Sean can hear a quiet sobbing.

It's 10:30 in the morning.

3

"They phoned me at work," his mother says.

A bottle of wine sits between them.

"I came home first. I don't know why. I was going to call your sister home from school, but I didn't. I went to the hospital, and they already had him in intensive care. It was close. Very close. I finally got in to see him, and he looked like another person. Someone else."

She raises her glass to her lips.

You nearly got rid of him, he thinks.

4

"He could die," he says.

"I don't care," says his sister.

He wonders what she's thinking, what she feels. He has no picture of how she sees herself, her relationships, her role, her future.

"I really don't," she says.

He nods. No matter what he says, she'll think he's contradicting her. I'm with you, he wants to say, but she wouldn't believe him.

He asks, "What are you doing tonight?"

"Going to a party."

She waits for him to say something. When he doesn't, she gives him a quizzical look.

"Can you buy me some beer?"

5

His father's girlfriend is on the phone.

"He wanted me to call you," he says.

"I'm sorry what happened, Sean, but it's over."

"He wants to see you," he says.

"It's over," she says.

6

The hockey game's on. They order a pitcher of beer.

"Did you hear? Kotsopolous's brother got shot," his friend says. "Nothing happened. He was alright."

Sean asks how.

"He was working at a doughnut shop."

"Someone shot him robbing a doughnut shop?"

"Yeah."

They laugh.

7

He can't sleep.

In the morning his father goes under the knife. Triple bypass surgery. They'll cut him up the middle, saw open his chest, peel back his ribs. Give him new arteries. Give him new life. Feed his heart with fresh blood. Revive him.

Sean rolls over, feels his erection, pulls and pulls and pulls.

8

"Tell your father he's dead," the kid said.

"If he touches my sister again, he's dead. I'll kill him, okay? You tell him."

He has Sean backed against the stairwell. Rumour has it one of the cashiers stood up to his father. Finally.

"I'll tell him," he says.

"I'll kill you, too," the kid says.

Sean sits in the hospital's cafeteria, watching the nurse at the next table finish her ice cream.

9

"She's never home," his mother says.

The surgery was successful. His father is sedated. He should be conscious in the morning, the doctors said. Sean sits with his mother in their kitchen. His sister has disappeared.

"She always comes back," his mother says. "But she never tells me where she's been."

10

They're in church. His sister, too. His mother rises to tell the congregation that her husband is still alive. The operation prolonged his life. The preacher gives thanks. The organ sounds. The congregation prays.

He excuses himself, walks out of the church and across the street, orders coffee at a twenty-four-hour café. The weekend paper sits on the counter. A woman was raped and killed in the west end. Stabbed twelve times through the torso. The police have charged a neighbour, a forty-five-year-old man with no criminal record. Father of two. Recently divorced.

11

His aunt visits, his father's sister.

"How's school going?"

They sit in the living room, sipping tea. His mother passes a plate of cookies. He tells his aunt he likes his professors. The campus is beautiful. And the mountains, he can't say enough about the mountains.

12

His sister brought her boyfriend home.

"It's my life!" she screams.

His mother slams her hand down on the table. She has no more words. It's my house, it's my house. His sister spins and slips out the side door. Her boyfriend stands waiting in the driveway, smoking a cigarette. His mother watches them out the window.

13

Two days before Christmas, the hospital releases his father. He sits up in bed in his housecoat, the morning paper beside him, a tray with juice, toast and fruit across his knees.

"This has been some adventure," his father says.

Sean asks him if he would like some coffee.

"No," his father says. "But thanks."

THE LAST MAN ON EARTH

Not long after I'm laid off, I approach the superintendent of my building.

"If you need anything done," I say.

"I'll keep you in mind," he promises.

A couple of days later one of my neighbours passes on.

Bernie calls me, says George is getting married.

"George is getting married?" It's the first I've heard from Bernie in a solid two years.

Bernie tells me about a stag for George.

"Can you be there?"

"No problem."

I forget to ask who's the bride.

The dead guy lived across the hall and two doors down. He wasn't old. I don't think. But he looked like hell. We were on chatting terms. We would nod to each other in the hall. One time we struck up a conversation in the laundry room. The laundry room has a couple of chairs and a ratty blue couch. I went down to plug another set of quarters into the dryer and found him spread out on the couch, flipping through one of the old magazines someone had left in a pile on the floor.

"Bitch, eh," he said. "That machine."

"Yeah, it's a bitch."

"It's a piece of shit," he said. "That thing."

I plugged my quarters into the machine. Went back upstairs.

Let me tell you about George.

The summer after high school he calls me. It's the middle of July. I'm working at a burger place, working my ass off. Working as many hours as they'll give me. I'm saving money. I'm going to university in September. George calls me. Says he needs to talk.

"I'm working," I say. "Can't talk right now. Call me later."

"Don't you care what I'm going through?"

I hang up.

Three hours at the Employment Centre signing forms. Snow falls and falls, while the clock spins. I come home to find a note stuffed under my door. It's from the super. Am I interested in cleaning out the dead guy's apartment?

Seems he had no one. Now no one wants his stuff.

Sort it out. Pack it up. Carry it off. That's the offer.

I find the superintendent and tell him I need the money.

Bernie's father has a couple of canoes, so George gets Bernie to organize a trip. It's late September. I have assignments, essays, exams, but I go. Bernie tells me it's going to be a dry trip. Two days paddling. Fresh air. Rocks. Water. The splendour of the forest. Winter imminent. I pack long underwear. George packs vodka.

We paddle, portage, paddle. Pitch camp. Light a fire. Drink.

George starts talking. He tells a couple I haven't heard before. One about Susan. One about Cindy. Then he starts talking about his father.

"When I was a kid, he used to hit me," he says. "He would tell me that I was useless, and then hit me. Across the mouth—smack!—with the back of his hand. I would run to my mother and bawl.

"Man, did I cry," he says.

He tells us how his mother told him his father beat him for his own good. How much he wanted to please his father. How he hates him now.

The superintendent gives me the key and I'm inside the dead guy's apartment. I bring a six–pack and a pair of work gloves. The apartment is small, a bachelor's, similar to my own. I twist open a beer and walk over to the window.

If you asked me, I'd probably say that George is the last man on earth.

Saturday night. I'm back from six months in Europe. George calls, tells me he's taken a job at one of the local malls. Assistant manager at a sporting goods store.

"What are you doing?"

"Nothing."

"I'll pick you up," he says. We cruise. I watch George work the bar. I order a rye and Coke. George introduces Samantha, Wendy, and Joan.

The dead guy's apartment. Piles and piles of paper. I open boxes, empty drawers. Paper. Paper. Paper. Hundreds of poems scrawled in a half-dead hand.

I read through the evening and into the night.

Poems about love. Poems about war. Poems about poverty, sickness, betrayal. I open another beer and dip into another box.

George's face disappears into her crotch. The icing runs up his nose. Bernie slaps him on the back. Stag night.

"That's the last free pussy for you," Bernie laughs.

George goes down for more.

A True Classless Future

Between the bank towers a hawk flew. Samuel watched the
bird from his office on the forty-fifth floor. It was the first
time he had seen a hawk there, in the space between the
bank's twin towers. For a second he thought it must be lost,
but then he remembered a story in yesterday's, Tuesday's,
paper. The city had introduced hawks into the downtown
core in an attempt to control the pigeon population. The
pigeons had no natural predators. Like bankers, thought
Samuel. Free to shit over everything.

He took a sip from his coffee and stared at his computer.
Five minutes earlier the machine had turned itself off. He
would have to call somebody, but so far he hadn't. The hawk
soared past his window again. Samuel watched it disappear
around the other side of the building. He reached for his
phone and called the switchboard.

They pledged to send someone right away.

Samuel picked a novel off his desk. He had a book
review to write. Five Hundred words. He had promised to
keep it short, but he found he had a lot to say. The book was
set in Europe in the late 1980s. The book's protagonist was a

window washer in Czechoslovakia who had been the editor of a small literary publication during the 1968 Prague Spring. He had published some articles critical of communism and when the Soviet tanks had rolled into his country later that year he had protested in the streets, only to be locked in jail for ten years. When he was finally released, he was forbidden to publish anything, and given a job as a window washer. A practical occupation. He was working for the people, acting out literally his heart's desire: to help his countrymen see the world more clearly.

The book followed this old man through the 1989 revolution, the one he had been waiting for all his life, and showed him on the other side, free of his oppressors, but at a loss for direction. The structure that had dominated his life had been taken away from him. Yes, he had wanted to be free of it, but had he ever expected this day to come? The book ended with his feeling betrayed by the new freedoms. They had come too late for him. It was a new world, and it had no place for him.

Samuel placed the book back on his desk. He hadn't been born until after the Russian tanks had come. He tried to place himself back in those times. He thought about what life must have been like before World War II, before the atomic bomb, the Berlin Wall, television. He knew about prohibition, segregated baseball, the Trotsky Trials, boxcar hoboes, the Beats, but he had no image of eastern Europe before the Russian invasion that drove out the Nazis. The Soviets were the liberators then. People must have been glad to see them. Some were even glad for the communism the Russians brought with them. It wasn't fascism. It wasn't what Hitler had brought. But the regimes turned crusty. The artists and intellectuals were silenced. The church was ridiculed. The window washer in the book had spent evening after evening in secret meetings with his friends, discussing how to bring down the regime, how to fight back. His life became consumed with the thought of acquiring freedom, but after the 1989 revolution the window washer's life did not change. He did not begin all the writing projects he had planned. Instead he walked around Prague, spitting on the advertising that had sprung up promoting consumer items he saw no need for and couldn't afford besides. "We're slaves to a new god," he told his comrades.

Samuel had met the woman who assigned him the book review at a party a month ago. Sarah had introduced him to her. It was Sarah's party. She was embarking on a trip around the world for an international environmental agency. Over the next six months she would be seeing most of the world's largest ecological disasters, some on the edge of collapse, others that had been brought back from the brink. He and Sarah had lived together during their last year of university. Sarah had helped him get his job at the bank. Her father was a senior manager. The book review editor, a short, dark-haired woman whom Samuel imagined to be roughly his own age (twenty-four), had touched him on the back of his hand and said, "I hear that you're a writer."

"Yes. I guess that's true." He wasn't in the habit of telling people.

"Sarah says you have some stories you'd like to publish."

"I have some stories," he said. "But I'm not sure that they're ready to be published—or that I'm ready to have them published."

The editor scolded him for being timid. How did he expect to get anywhere? Maybe he would like to write a book review for her. As a way of getting started. She gave him her business card (which he promptly lost—what was her name?) and told him to call her on Monday. She would send him a book to review.

Samuel looked at his notes. He had written down passages he considered particularly meaningful.

page 31
Pavel walked home from the meeting through familiar streets

*made strange by the heavy fog, his heart buoyed by the group's
plans. Too much time had been spent these past months talking. It
was time for action.*

page 150
 *The room seemed to close in on him. His books lifted
themselves off the shelves and floated about the room. They were
all useless now. All the ideas he had so eagerly stuffed into his
head. What had they changed? What was different? The books
spun in a circle above his head, tormenting him with the power he
had given them.*

There was a knock on the door. Samuel turned around
to see a man in a suit standing in the doorway, holding a
briefcase. He had a crewcut.
 "Problem with your computer?"
 Samuel nodded. He pointed to it as if to identify the
culprit.
 The man walked over to the machine and wiped the dust
off its screen.
 After a brief initial investigation, he said he would like to
open it up and poke around.
 "It'll probably take about half an hour."
 "I'll take some work down to the cafeteria," said Samuel.
"I've got a break coming." He picked up his notes, a couple
of folders and the novel, and walked down the hallway to the
elevator.

He first met Sarah in a history class they shared. They
worked together on a lab project, a presentation on the 1837
Upper Canada Rebellion. By the end of the project she had
convinced him that she was the most organized, literate,
creative, vital person he had ever met. She took charge from
the beginning, bringing stacks of books she had dug out of

the library to each meeting they held. She planned their presentation almost to the second, but she didn't dominate. She asked him for his contributions and considered all his suggestions, integrating many of them into the final project. They did extremely well and they were both pleased.

A month later he ran into her at a party. She was standing with her back against a wall in the hallway, her long, blonde hair hanging down and covering her face, a beer bottle dangling out of one hand. He stood beside her for a minute before she turned to see who was there. "Hug me," she said, her voice trailing away behind the dance music pounding out of the basement. He walked her home through the light snow and put her to bed, then lay down beside her on top of the covers and listened to her mumble about how she hated herself, how her parents hated her, how her brothers hated her, how her classmates and professors hated her. "The only creature who doesn't hate me is my dog," she said. "And she's dead."

There was six inches of snow on the ground the next morning. She rose before him and began frying bacon and eggs. She brought him a glass of orange juice, and toast covered with marmalade on a plate shared with slices of apple and pear. She rubbed his forehead and kissed him on the cheek.

As they walked to school together that morning she told him about her family, her father the banker, her mother the school board administrator (she had previously been a teacher). She was the youngest of three, the baby and the only girl. She started calling him every couple of days, but neither seemed ready to discuss the possibility of a relationship. Sarah had a boyfriend out of the country. They had been going together since she was sixteen. He was older than her, she said. Samuel wasn't sure how much. She went to Europe over Christmas to see him.

Samuel spent the holidays trying not to think about her. When he returned to school, he called her, but her roommate said she hadn't come back. Three weeks later he got a letter from Spain, saying she was coming home. It hadn't worked out with her boyfriend. She called him a couple of days later. She had a job waitressing at a small café and a room in a boarding house. She invited him over for tea and told him the story.

Her boyfriend owned a hotel in a tourist town along the Mediterranean. He had promised to leave his wife for her. He had been sending her love letters since she was sixteen, when she had met him in his hotel on a school-organized European visit. Her parents thought she had turned the head of some young man on the beach and often teased her about her Latin lover. But Pablo was nearing fifty and getting paunchy. How he had managed to get her into bed that first time, she couldn't remember.

"He said I was the smartest woman he had ever met," she told Samuel. "He said Spanish women were crafty, full of lies and trickery because they were weak. They didn't know how to think. He said I was the best lover he had ever had. He said that, I'm sure, because he knew the first time I slept with him I was a virgin."

She said all this in a flat, matter-of-fact voice, as she offered him more tea. He wanted to tell her he had missed her, but he listened instead for two hours until she sighed and looked him in the eyes.

"I have been bad to you, haven't I?" she asked.

He shook his head. "No."

"I have, I know I have. You don't have to lie to me. I like you, too, but I couldn't be with you before. I had to end this thing with Pablo. And now I have."

The elevator opened and Samuel turned the corner into the cafeteria. He walked the length of the room between the empty tables, and bought a coffee and a muffin. In half an hour the room would be nearly full, ringing with the chatter of conversations about stock prices, baseball scores and rumoured office affairs. He found a table near the window and sat down.

The last time he had heard from Sarah she was in Guatemala, trying to save the rainforest. He hadn't known they had any rainforest in Guatemala. Wasn't that Brazil? She was living in the jungle with a group of aging hippies and young eco-fascists. Like herself, she wrote. They were trying to convince the local authorities to stop turning the jungle into grazing land for cattle. They were promoting eco-tourism as an alternative source of income. The authorities were sceptical. Rich Americans would come to the jungle? They would come if they thought they were helping to save the planet. But it's just a jungle. No, no, no. It's a primitive ecosystem, a geographic wonder, a rare and precious commodity, the source of many yet–uncovered discoveries. The cure for cancer may be in there. But the authorities weren't buying it, so Sarah's group had begun building alliances with the aboriginal peoples. They understood the value of the land, the danger of money.

Her tour was scheduled to shift to Peru in the week after she wrote, but she had said she was so caught up with the situation in Guatemala she might stay there. He hadn't heard from her since.

It was like that with her. How many times had they sat down on a Friday night to try to figure out their itinerary, only to start again a dozen times, then a dozen times after that? How many sweaters had she bought and returned? She even had trouble picking out a meal at McDonald's. Her father said she got it from her mother, her mother said she was in a league of her own.

After a rough start, Samuel had come to enjoy Sarah's parents. Sarah invited him to a dinner party. They arrived in jeans and t-shirts. Everyone else was stuffed into black ties and evening gowns. Her father was hosting investors from

New York. He remembered feeling the blush on his face as he spoke to an elegant older woman who had probably spent as much on her hair as he had paid a few days earlier for a month's rent. He wore a black t-shirt and had recently cut his hair. She kept asking him if he was a beatnik. "You can't be a hippie, your hair's too short."

"And he's not a punk," said another woman. "He would have orange hair if he were a punk."

"He doesn't need to have orange hair to be a punk," said her husband.

Out of the corner of his eye Samuel could see Sarah gesticulating wildly as she tried to explain to a large balding man with shaggy jowls, who Samuel later learned owned a supermarket chain, how beef farming was sucking up all of America's ground water, while he nodded and stared at her chest.

"Sarah was the golden child," her father told him later. "The baby, of course. We gave her everything she wanted. She enjoyed the benefits of our stability that the boys missed. Our world was so full of optimism when she was younger. It's a dangerous thing to tell a child, that anything is possible. When they see all the problems in the world, they want to fix them."

"I would have turned out this way anyway, Daddy." Sarah came up behind him and kissed him on the temple. "The world needs people like me."

Her father smiled at her. "Yes it does," he said. "But you make life difficult for people like me."

They stepped between a pair of glass doors into the backyard. An extensive rock garden, which Sarah's mother had spent years perfecting, filled the left side of the yard. Punctuated with statues from sculptors she admired, it paraded a mixture of wildflowers and cultivated plants. A water fountain poured into a small pond at the back of the yard beside a gazebo. Sarah's father led them to a park bench on the right side of the yard, which backed onto a small, rectangular slab of concrete, the boys' basketball court. The yard's only concession to modern family life.

"Sarah was a precocious girl," began her father. "Brilliant actually. She was a whiz in school early on. Far ahead of her brothers in that respect. But the wheels came off when she hit puberty. We weren't quite sure what to do with her after that."

Sarah had wandered down to the water fountain. She turned back to her father. "What happened to the goldfish?"

"Died. Last fall. We left them in too long." He turned to Samuel. "Froze to death, the poor buggers."

Samuel nodded.

"And you, young man," Sarah's father said. "What's up for you?"

"I'm finishing off my degree."

"Yes. And then? Got the travel bug?"

He shook his head. "I don't think I can afford it."

Sarah's father pulled out a pack of cigarettes and offered one to Samuel, who turned it down.

"You young people," Sarah's father said. "Not our boys. They've done all right. But you and Sarah. I don't know if I'd want to live in your world." He took a drag on his cigarette. "The Cold War's over and all that. Communism's gone, thank god. And even South Africa appears to be putting things right. But those old rules were easy to live by. We knew who the enemy was. Now, who knows? Maybe Sarah's right. Maybe it's us, with our pollution and global warming. But do you ever hear anything about acid rain any more? Seems to me we licked that and we can lick these other things, too."

"I don't understand," said Samuel.

"What don't you understand, son?"

"Why wouldn't you want to be young again?"

"The rules, my friend. There's no more rules. You've got to stand up and take your chance, but you can have it taken from you at any second. I've seen it happen. You never know when things are going to change."

From the other end of the cafeteria Samuel saw Scott
walking toward him. Scott worked in the kitchen. They had
been buddies in high school. The day he had looked up to
see Scott in his white cotton uniform, he had nearly sent his
lunch flying across the room. He had stood there in his blue
blazer and new silk tie. They hadn't seen each other in five
years.

Scott pulled up a chair opposite him.

He picked up the novel. "What are you doing with this?"

"Book review."

"For Daddy upstairs?"

"No. A fiction magazine. I met this woman at Sarah's
party. An editor."

"Right. Listen." He stood up and patted Samuel on the
shoulder. "The boys are going out for some brews after
work. You want to come?"

"Sure."

"Great. See you at five."

People were starting to arrive for their coffee break.
Samuel looked out the window and watched the sparrows
pick up crumbs underneath the picnic tables in the
courtyard. Ugly birds. Small, brown, bland birds. Can't carry
a tune. They're not even meant to be here. Brought over by
some lunatic Brit who thought Canada ought to have all the
same species as the Old Country. Or was that starlings? The
ferocious ugly bird. Ate its young. He couldn't remember.

He thought about the hawk he had seen that morning. It
wasn't meant to be here, either. It was brought in to kill off
the pigeons. But if you got rid of the buildings, got rid of the
skyscrapers, the towers, factories, warehouses,
condominiums, sports stadiums, and brought in a forest and
a few meadows, then the hawk would be right at home. It
was just trying to survive like everybody else.

He finished his coffee and collected his things.

Upstairs his computer was spread across his desk.

He walked down the hall to find an empty office.

"Nothing to this job," Sarah's father had said. "All you have to do is read the crap our analysts have written and clean it up a bit. Turn it into English. You'll know what to do when you see it."

He had sat down at his desk that first day, flipped through a pile of reports and felt his head begin to throb. Turn it into English. No problem.

No one was in the meeting room so he dumped his work papers on the end of the table and made himself comfortable.

Ten years the window washer had spent in prison. Ten years of scribbling down notes, making outlines for plays, jotting down and revising thousands of poems. Stacks and stacks of notebooks he had piled up in his cell. Five volumes of poetry, three plays, two unfinished novels. Then one day he asked the guards to take them away. They were a burden to him. He asked them to take away his books, too. Plus his box of letters. Everything but a change of clothes. He wanted nothing. He wanted to stop believing in illusions. He wanted only the bare walls and his bed. The bars, the floor, a mattress and a blanket. They could take the pillow. What use was a pillow? Such extravagance! For six months he stopped talking to anyone until he woke up one morning crying and couldn't stop. They took him to the infirmary and told him if he didn't pull himself together they would send him to the asylum. He asked for his books back and his poems, but they told him they had burned them. A month later they opened the prison doors and pushed him outside.

One of the secretaries appeared in the doorway.

"A call for you. Line two."

The book editor. Party tonight. A small club on Queen Street was hosting a reading. A gaggle of young poets. That's what she said. Gaggle. Should be interesting. Poetry's back, you know.

"From where?" he asked.

"From wherever it goes when it goes away. To a South

Sea island where it suns itself and gets ready for its big comeback. Like Marlon Brando."

"Is he back, too?"

"Oh yes. Marlon's back. And he's bigger than ever."

He said he would be there, as soon as he got away from the dish pigs.

At five he stood inside the front doors, thirsting.

Scott arrived and led him to a strip club two blocks away.

The first woman came out to the strains of Steppenwolf's "Born to be Wild."

Shane and Derrick sat opposite them.

Samuel and Scott talked their way into their first strip club when they were seventeen. What a crazy year that had been! Scott's fifteen-year-old sister got pregnant. Samuel's parents were firing missiles across the city at each other, handing him letter bombs to carry back and forth. No one paid any attention to two seventeen–year–olds out for a good time, eager to find a place that was their's alone.

The second stripper's name was Mindy. She was writhing on the stage on a blanket when their beers arrived.

"What about you?" said Scott, turning to Samuel. "Any action on the home front?"

"None."

"You're not still hung up on Sarah, are you?"

Samuel shook his head as Mindy left the stage and passed in front of them.

Scott had been there the night Samuel lost his virginity, the night of the bonfire. It was part of their crazy summer. The series of parties that ended the schoolyear led up to a bash in the valley. Samuel stumbled with a girl into the trees. They lay down beside a fallen log, eased themselves onto a bed of broken twigs and wet leaves. She was two years older than him. He had met her on the street two weeks earlier with a mutual friend. She produced a condom, put him in her. She warned him not to make demands of her. As it turned out, he never saw her again. But he kept asking about her until Scott teased him silent.

Scott pointed his thumb at Samuel and said to the others, "He's lovesick."

"That true?" asked Shane.

Samuel looked at the stripper on the stage.

"No," he said. "I'm just sensitive, you know."

"Where's your ponytail?"

"I cut it off to sell my soul at the bank."

"Welcome to how the other half lives," Derrick said. He swung his eyes to the stage.

Shane leaned across the table. "You can't let women control you," he said. "Because they will, you know. If you give them the chance. Take this guy I know. He gets married and his wife won't let him out of the house. The only time he goes out is to go to work, make some money, but then he doesn't get to spend it. I tell you, some regular pussy is not worth that."

Samuel didn't say anything. He edged out of the booth and left in search of the bathroom. Samuel saw that he was about to be cast as "the man with the broken balls" while he watched women take off their clothes and dry fuck a blanket. Let them cast me any way they want, he thought. He didn't have the energy to fight it.

The boys were talking about baseball when he returned. The home team had won the World Series the year before, their first time, and they appeared destined to repeat, though they had slumped the last few games.

A stripper stopped at their booth and asked them if they wanted a table dance. Shane and Derrick shook their heads, no. Samuel nodded, yes. He wanted them to know he was having a good time. He wanted them to know that he could do it.

"Thanks, man," Scott said, when she was gone. "You get

a little extra cash working upstairs, eh? Good for a few perks now and then."

He didn't want to tell him about his student loan. He liked the attention. He was sure Scott had no idea what his life was like now. He hadn't told him and Scott hadn't asked. When they met they stuck to what seemed to be a few select and safe topics. Women. Sports. The past. When the selection had been made, Samuel wasn't sure, but the categories became clearer every time they talked.

Half an hour later they were out on the street. They shook hands and parted. Samuel stopped for a slice of pizza on his way to the book editor's party. Twilight was beginning to settle on the city. The streets were busy. The cafés were crowded. He walked along Queen Street until he found the club. The book editor had her back against the bar. She stepped out between an arguing couple to greet him.

"Did you hear what happened today?" she asked.

"No."

"A woman was raped on a commuter train."

"That's terrible."

"People are wearing black to remember." She pointed to her dress.

"People around here are always wearing black." It was out before he could stop it.

"We have a lot to remember," she said.

Saving the world through fashion design, Samuel thought. Brave souls.

"Thanks for coming," the book editor said. She brushed her fingers across his chest and led him to a table near the stage. He found himself looking at the women and wondering what they looked like under their clothes. Strip clubs had that effect on him.

He noticed the book editor's body for the first time.

It had been almost a year since he had been with a woman. Sarah had become increasingly unhappy and decided she wanted more space. It had been an amicable split and they had slept together a half–dozen times since the official end of their relationship. He still found it hard to stir up interest in other women.

The reading started almost an hour late. Samuel thought of the window washer. What would he have thought of this? The designer beers, the activist fashion: they seemed a weak foundation for art, great or otherwise. Samuel ordered another beer. He felt like he'd had too much to drink, but it was too early to feel that way.

The poets entertained and provoked. The first poet, a woman, spat out lesbian angst and lust. A second woman followed. She jumped around the stage, pausing now and again to shout out single abrupt phrases. Examples of international injustice. "East Timor." "Palestine." "South Central LA." She looked like a spider caught in a web. Maybe that was the point, Samuel thought. She's stuck in a corrupt world. The third poet, a man, stood behind the microphone and read a long poem about the death of BC's coastal rain forests in a monotone voice that got increasingly louder. The poem was uninterrupted by syntax or any discernible rhythm. After the first thirty seconds Samuel turned his attention to the book editor, who appeared fixated on the speaker. Was any of this changing anything? Would the world be a better place because of this reading? Samuel knew these were the wrong questions to ask. Poetry was its own meaning. But the poets had raised the questions themselves. They had wanted to inform, to prod, ultimately to change the external circumstances of the world.

Later, he walked the book editor to her apartment. The night was starting to cool down, but it was still warm. They passed a couple pushing a baby stroller.

"I have something for you," she said.

He wished he could remember her name.

"The author of the book you're reviewing is going to be here next week for a conference. The organizers sent me a pair of tickets."

"Great," he said. He was excited. "Will there be time for questions?"

"Probably." She nodded. She slipped her arm around his. He felt her breast against his arm. She laughed.

"You used to go out with Sarah, didn't you?"

"We lived together for a year."

"Really." She sounded surprised. She turned down a side street and led him across the lawn of the third house in from the corner. The house was divided into three separate living spaces. She lived alone upstairs. He followed her to her apartment and sat on the couch while she turned on the stereo and put on a Charlie Parker CD.

"Bird's great," said Samuel.

"Who?"

"Charlie Parker. Bird. That was his nickname."

"Oh, is that who this is? I just like the music. Jazz is so sexy. Hold on while I get the tickets."

She left the room.

A lava lamp sat on the table at the end of the couch beside Samuel. He hadn't seen one of those in ages. A poster of Van Gogh's *Starry Night* hung on the opposite wall. The coffee table was buried in books, presumably new releases awaiting review. A copy of the latest *Rolling Stone* lay beside them. Samuel was flipping through it when the book editor returned with the tickets. She had changed into an oversized cotton blouse. She handed him the tickets and asked him if he wanted anything to drink.

"Only if you're having something," he said.

She disappeared again into what Samuel had thought was the bedroom and returned with two tumblers full of a rich red wine. After she handed him his wine she sat on the couch with her back against the wall and her feet in Samuel's lap, her deeply tanned bare legs stretched out in front of her. She pulled her feet off his lap and stuck her toes underneath his thigh.

"It gets chilly in here at night," she said.

"I bet that's a lie."

She laughed. The previous week had been unbearably muggy.

"So you lived with Sarah," she said at last.

"Yes."

"Did that end when she started seeing Mark?"

"Who?"

"Mark. You know, the guy she's on this trip with."

Samuel felt something turn over in his stomach.

"No. It was before that," he said, but it was too late.

"She never told you? You don't know?"

"We broke up a year ago."

"But she never told you why?"

"She wanted more space."

"Shit," she said. "That woman never ceases to amaze."

He asked, "How do you know Sarah?"

"We went to school together, junior high and high school."

"Were you close?"

"The closest."

"She never mentioned you," he said. He began massaging her ankles.

"That doesn't surprise me," she said. "We had a falling out after she got pregnant."

Samuel stopped what he was doing.

"Sarah was pregnant?"

"Sure. You didn't know that, either?"

"When was this?"

"The first year of university. She had an abortion."

Two years before I found her bawling at that party, Samuel thought.

The book editor picked herself up and jumped into his lap. "But let's not talk about that," she said, rubbing her fingers through his hair. She brought her face in close to his and kissed him. He placed his hand on her thigh to shift her weight more comfortably and kissed her back. She smiled and started unbuttoning his shirt.

When he finally got home, well after midnight, he hauled his tired body and throbbing head into his apartment to find a letter from Sarah. He pulled a chair out from the kitchen table and poured himself a glass of orange juice. He grabbed a knife and slid it into the envelope.

The world is dying, Sarah wrote from Australia. She was living in the outback with a group of aborigines. They were teaching her the natural ways of the earth. There was no mention of anyone named Mark. Samuel began to wonder if the book editor hadn't been lying. As he read the letter he felt Sarah in the rhythm of the sentences, in her choice of words, in her jokes. He felt his love for her. This is the woman he knew, the one he had fallen in love with, the one who wanted to save the world.

The next morning the bank was abuzz. The international currency markets had shifted overnight. Samuel spent the day amidst a flurry of activity as people rushed from department to department, shuffling papers and pointing at computer screens. (His own was nowhere to be seen.) There was a message on his answering machine when he got in later in the day. From Lauren, the book editor. (That was her name!) She asked him if he had any plans, then said she had heard a rumour that Sarah was back in town. Click. He picked up the phone and called her. The line was busy.

Doug, his roommate, was sitting on the couch in his underwear and tennis socks, watching a rerun of "Miami Vice" on one of the satellite channels and nursing a Coke. He held a bowl of popcorn between his knees.

"You look awful," Doug said.

Samuel calculated what it would take to remove Doug's two front teeth and decided the result wasn't worth the effort or the risk. Doug would exact revenge. Put vinegar in his contact lens solution. Besides, the man was armed. Doug owned a dozen guns of various sizes. Most of them he kept loaded.

Samuel called Lauren again.

"Oh, hi," she said after picking up the phone on the seventh ring. "I'm glad you called. Did you work late tonight?"

"A little. It was chaos all day."

"Listen, I'm having some people over."

Was that a question?

"I'll be there," he said. "When?"

"Nine or ten," she said.

"Great. I'm going to take a nap."

"Don't oversleep," she teased.

"I won't."

"I miss you."

"You're wonderful." What was he saying? They hung up. Did he like this girl? He did, he did, but where had she come from? How had she gotten to him so fast? He hadn't had time to think about the previous night. Then there was Sarah's letter. Wait. Lauren had said that Sarah might be back. He had forgotten to ask her about it. He would do it later. Right now all he wanted to do was sleep. He told Doug he was going to take a nap and Doug told him he was going out.

The apartment became suddenly quiet.

He pulled off his shoes and threw off his tie. He slid under the covers. The faucet in the kitchen was dripping. Some kids were playing outside. He closed his eyes.

Two hours later, the phone rang. It was Lauren.

"I thought you might need a wake–up call," she said.

He grumbled an inarticulate thank you. His eyes were stuck shut. He peeled them open. He had forgotten to take out his contacts.

It was five minutes after nine.

"I'll be over shortly," he said. "Should I bring anything?"

"Just yourself."

I'll get some wine, he thought. No. Flowers.

He shed his clothes and stepped into the shower. Ten minutes later he threw his cashmere jacket on over a t-shirt and a pair of jeans and sneakers. Cross–dressing, he thought. No–nonsense style. He felt better. Refreshed. He called a cab.

Lauren took the flowers and kissed him. She put them in a vase, set the lava lamp on the floor and replaced it with the flowers. She poured Samuel a glass of sherry, kissed him on the neck and wrapped her arms around him. No one else had arrived yet. They moved over to the couch.

At eleven he asked her if anyone was coming.

"Probably not. They said they might, but—"

"If they're not here by now," he said.

"Right."

He stood up and put on a Miles Davis CD. Lauren came to him and slid off her top. He unbuttoned his jeans. Afterwards, he fell asleep and slipped into a dream.

He was at Sarah's cottage in the bedroom where they had made love for the first time. The bed was unmade. A fire burned in the wood stove. He heard her voice, laughter coming from the bathroom. He turned toward the open door. Sarah stood before the mirror, fixing her hair, a dark towel wrapped around her body. She was talking to someone. He moved closer. He stepped into the bathroom, slid open the shower.

"What's the matter?"

He opened his eyes. He was sitting up. Lauren rubbed his back.

"Hey," she said. "Lie down. What happened?"

"Bad dream," he said. He shook himself as if to throw off a spirit.

She pushed him onto his side and snuggled up to his back. Her arm wrapped around him, she rubbed her fingers gently across his chest.

She succeeded in inducing an erection.

The alarm went off hours later. He groaned, but she pulled him out of bed and dragged him into the shower. He couldn't believe he was involved with a morning person. Later, he walked with her to a bank machine to get money for cab fare, then rushed home and off to work.

"Did you really hear that Sarah was back?" he asked before leaving her.

"Yes."

"From a reliable source?"

"Very."

His day went much like the day before. People started calling, asking for their reports. He said that he hadn't seen his computer in two days. They sent their secretaries down for his hard copy. They would make the changes themselves. If they bothered at all.

The hawk sailed past his window.

The phone rang. It was Lauren.

"Busy?"

"Much," he said.

"There's a party tonight. At a warehouse in the west end."

"Great."

"Okay?" She sounded unsure.

"Yes. Fine. Sorry, was I being distant?"

"Yes."

"You caught me in the middle of something," he said. "Do you want to meet me for dinner later?"

"That would be nice."

He met her at the corner of Queen and Spadina in the heart of Chinatown. They found a small hole-in-the-wall restaurant and sat sipping green tea and playing with their chopsticks.

"You look washed out," she said.

He asked her what she meant.

"I don't know. Like a watercolour dipped in the bathtub. You've lost your edges."

"I'm tired."

"You're worn down," she agreed.

Their food arrived. Samuel poked at one dish with his chopsticks.

"What's this?" he asked.

"That's the squid," said Lauren. "I think."

"The squid?" He didn't remember ordering squid. He pulled off a piece and dropped it in his mouth. A salty, fishy taste. Not bad. He reached back for more.

She asked, "How's the book review coming?"

"I was hoping you'd forgotten about it."

"No, no. I'd never do that." She looked at him, smiling, and raised her eyebrows. "So?"

He smiled.

"You're beautiful," he said.

She laughed.

"Your edges are coming back," she said.

"Oh good."

Their server returned to refill their tea.

"I've started it," he said.

"Good."

"I liked it, the book, but I'm not clear on some of its conclusions."

"Like what?"

"Like the moral ambiguity about the end of communism."

"What's ambiguous about it?"

"Life doesn't improve after it's gone."

"No?" she asked.

"Not really. Not for the protagonist. It does in general, I think. And he's quite clear that freedom of expression is now fully accepted. But the lives of the ordinary people continue much as they had before. It's like here. That's what I'm thinking. Most people don't care about politics; they just want a job, some spending money, some free time. They want to be safe. They want to be able to do what they want, when they want to do it."

"But that's what communism wouldn't allow."

"True," he said. "But I think a lot of that is an illusion here as well. People here do what the government wants. They do what their companies want. People who question how things work are marginalized. They're not put in jail or anything like that, but it's easy to draw a parallel between our inability to question 'the system' and the problem of poets in the former Eastern Block."

"Well, all right," she said. "But you're not going to put all that in the book review, are you?"

"No. You'd only edit it out."

She smiled. "That's right."

They paid their bill and caught a streetcar to the party.

They entered up an iron staircase at the back of the warehouse near what had once been the loading bay. A bar had been built along one wall. Wooden, ten-foot walls, stretching a third of the way to the ceiling, had been placed throughout the room to create separate sections. They all led into the middle, where lasers illuminated a dance floor. There was hardly anyone there. Lauren wasn't worried. She said she wanted him to meet some people, then they could leave and come back later if they wanted. They walked around the room, peering into dark corners until she found someone she recognized.

"Benoit! Charlene!"

Lauren took his hand and led him into the darkness. Benoit and Charlene sat crowded onto a dilapidated couch. Lauren and Samuel pulled up a pair of plastic chairs from a nearby pile.

Charlene leaned forward and tapped Samuel on the knee. "You know Sarah," she said. It sounded like a command.

"Yes. You too?"

"Oh yes." She threw her head back. "Sarah's an old friend."

They sat in silence for a moment, then Samuel asked Lauren if she wanted anything from the bar. A beer? A cooler? Lauren nodded.

"Whatever," she said.

"Excuse me," he said to Charlene. She stood up for a second and he thought she was going to come with him, but she just straightened her skirt, a black mini, unbuttoned her jacket and sat down again. She looked up at Samuel as he turned to go.

Did she blow him a kiss? He thought he had seen her purse her lips and blow him one on his way. Crazy scene. He shouldered up to the bar and ordered two beers.

He felt a hand on his shoulder.

"Buddy!"

It was Scott. "What are you doing here?"

"Same as you, pal. Cruising and hoping."

"How did you hear about this place?" Samuel asked.

"The secretary in the marketing department. She knows about all the happenings."

Two women appeared beside them at the bar.

"Here she is," said Scott. He introduced them as Kelly and Samantha.

Samuel told Scott that he was with Lauren.

"I'd love to meet her," Scott said.

Samuel led them through the darkness. When he found the couch, it was empty. Samuel squeezed onto the couch between Scott and Samantha.

"Sam's a technical writer," Scott said.

Samantha confirmed that this was her occupation as she opened a pack of cigarettes and pulled out a joint. She lit it, took a hit and passed it to Samuel. He took a hit and passed it to Scott.

"It's been a long time since I've had any of that," Samuel said.

"Really," Samantha said. "Why's that?"

He shrugged. "It's not a habit. I don't care for it too much."

"When was the last time?"

He thought about it. Scott passed the joint back to Samantha.

"Last year," Samuel said. "Before graduation a couple of us got together."

"Have you ever written anything while you were stoned?" Samantha asked.

"No. Have you?"

She nodded and smiled. She passed the joint back to him and he passed it to Scott.

"I was working on my thesis—it's on *Wuthering Heights*—and one night I sat down at my computer after smoking up and I started writing. After a while I stopped to read what I'd done and I thought, 'This is shit. It's full of ambiguities.' Everything I'd written had two or three meanings, so I started editing it. When I was done, I saved it and went to bed. The next day I turned on my computer and called up my file and found that I'd written: 'Emily Brontë wrote books.'"

They laughed. Samuel spit his beer on the floor.

"That's a great story," he said.

He was feeling good.

Someone stepped in front of him. He looked up. It was Lauren. He struggled to his feet and introduced everyone.

"Sarah was here," Lauren said. "There's a party at her place. Do you want to go?"

"No." It came out like a bullet. If she was back, he didn't want to meet her like this. He didn't want to walk in on a party that he hadn't been specifically invited to.

"No," he repeated. He tried to make it sound like he would rather be with her, but he sensed that Lauren wanted to go to the party. Benoit and Charlene appeared to have already left.

"Okay," he said, taking her by the hands. "But dance with me first."

She smiled and dragged him towards the dance floor. Samuel closed his eyes and tried to clear his head. He tried to think about Sarah as she had been when he first met her, when he realized that he was in love with her, when he had finally confronted the fact she had left him.

Lauren grabbed him gently by the shoulder. "Time to go."

Scott had been sent to find a taxi. Samuel followed Lauren and Samantha outside and piled behind them into the cab.

"Where is this place?" Scott asked.

When Lauren told him, he said, "I worked up there one summer on a gardening crew. Nice places."

Lauren wrapped her hand around Samuel's knee.

"Are you going to be okay?" she asked.

"Sure," he said. "No problem."

A party was indeed in progress when they arrived. Sixteen cars ringed the curved driveway. Music drifted out from the backyard.

Lauren led them around the side of the house.

Sarah's father stood in the middle of the yard, a cigar in one hand, a cocktail glass in the other, looking, Samuel thought, a little like Winston Churchill. There might have been fifty or sixty people standing in pockets around the yard. Scott followed Samantha to the drinks table. Lauren had her arms around a diminutive girl encircled by four gargantuan young men in rugby jerseys. Another old friend, thought Samuel. He didn't see Sarah anywhere. He had a sudden desire for a cigarette.

Scott returned from the drinks table and handed him a beer.

"Would you take a look at this place?"

"Careful now," Samuel scolded him.

Scott smiled and raised his beer to Samuel.

"Cheers," he said. They clinked their bottles together.

Samuel later remembered watching Lauren engage in a lively discussion with one of the rugby players. He remembered Scott telling him about the secretary in the marketing department, about her special gifts and the best way to ask for them. He remembered asking the diminutive girl if she knew Sarah. "Oh, sure," the girl had said. Did she know where she was? "Inside," the girl said. "Or she might have left already to go to the airport. Her boyfriend's coming in on a flight at midnight."

Her boyfriend? Mark?

"Oh, no," the girl had said. "That's Mark over there."

She pointed at a tall, thin man in a loosely fitting sports jacket and slacks.

"The new boyfriend's from Peru," the girl said, smiling. "He sells racehorses. At least, his family does. He's a TV actor, I think."

Samuel remembered watching her depart with three of the rugby players. He remembered tapping Mark on the shoulder and introducing himself.

"Oh, *that* Samuel," Mark had said.

Was it the alcohol? the marijuana earlier? the excitement? Samuel was uncertain of everything except one fact. He had never hit anyone before, never slugged anyone in his life before that night.

"Easy come, easy go," Mark had said, and Samuel had hit him. Mark had stepped back and then threw what remained of his cocktail in Samuel's face.

"I abhor violence," he said.

"I don't," Samuel said, and lunged at Mark again.

Samuel remembered passing Sarah's father, who looked at him silently, his cigar stuffed into the left corner of his mouth. The taxi arrived and Samuel left with Scott and Samantha. Where was Lauren? The taxi stopped in front of a small club on College. Samuel remembered finding a table in the back, the jazz on the audio system and one shot of Jack Daniels after that.

The next day, Friday, he called in sick and stayed home.

On Monday he repeated the procedure.

Then on Tuesday he did it again. Lauren hadn't called. She hadn't faxed, she hadn't e-mailed. Samuel finished the book review. He put it in an envelope, dropped it in the mailbox outside his apartment block, and took himself to the coffee shop on the corner. The book review had topped out at just under 1,200 words. "Marx's utopian philosophy may have proven a poor model for this century's communist dreamers," he had written. "Reality is a harsh teacher, but it remains true, as Lenin said, that if you want to make an omelette you have to break a few eggs. Ideals and utopian fantasies are the necessary fuel of the heart. The trick is to recognize the limitations of this world, the world of baseball, children and love affairs, the world of mutability, the world of despair. In wanting to make the world a better place, Marx forgot these limitations, and the dreamers who tried to make his fictions into fact created some of the worst horrors of the millennium. But let's not condemn all dreamers (or all dreams) for the failure of the communist utopia, and let's not stop dreaming of a true classless future." It was dreck, Samuel thought. Lauren would hate it. She would cut the review in half. No, more likely she wouldn't even read it.

He sat in the coffee shop, reading the newspaper. An eighteen-month-old baby girl had been found the night before, wandering on a downtown side street at two in the morning. She had apparently been left outside by her father, sleeping in a stroller, and had woken up and walked off. The father, who, according to the newspaper account, had sole custody of the child, was arrested when he returned home from drinking at a nearby watering hole. He reportedly said he thought the child had been with its mother.

Samuel read this story and sipped his coffee.

He made his way home and took two messages off his answering machine, one from his supervisor at the bank. The second from Samatha. He picked up the phone and started to dial.